"What I know, Mr. Nudger, is that Curtis didn't kill nobody."

"Curtis has exhausted all his appeals," Nudger said to this hopelessly naive girl-woman. "Even if all the witnesses changed their stories, it wouldn't necessarily mean he'd get a new trial."

"Maybe not, but I betcha they wouldn't kill him. They couldn't stand the publicity if enough witnesses said they was wrong, it was somebody else shot the old woman. Then, just maybe, eventually, Curtis would get another trial and get out of prison."

Nudger stared at her. He was awed. Here was foolish optimism that transcended even his own. He had to admire Candy Ann.

The shapely pale leg started pumping again beneath the cornflower-blue dress. When Nudger lowered his gaze to stare at it, Candy Ann said, "So will you help me, Mr. Nudger?"

"Sure," Nudger said, "It sounds easy."

Other Tor Books by John Lutz

JOHN LUTZ
RIDE THE LIGHTNING

TOR®

A TOM DOHERTY ASSOCIATES BOOK
NEW YORK

RIDE THE LIGHTNING

Published by arrangement with St. Martin's Press, Inc.

A TOR Book
Published by Tom Doherty Associates, Inc.
49 West 24 Street
New York, NY 10010

Cover art by Jeanette Adams

ISBN: 0-812-50642-1   Can. ISBN: 0-812-52643-X

Library of Congress Catalog Number: 86-27949

First Tor edition: January 1990

Printed in the United States of America

0 9 8 7 6 5 4 3 2 1

For I. Ingelsfeld, by any other name.

It is a fact—or have I dreamt it—that by means of electricity, the world of matter has become a great nerve, vibrating thousands of miles in a breathless point of time? Rather, the round globe is a vast head, a brain, instinct with intelligence: or shall we say it is itself a thought, nothing but thought, and no longer the substance which we dreamed it.

—Nathaniel Hawthorne
The House of the Seven Gables

This is a marvel of the universe
To fling a thought across a stretch of sky—
Some weighty message, or a yearning cry.

—Josephine L. Peabody
Wireless

A slanted sheet of rain swept like a scythe across Placid Grove Trailer Park. For an instant, an intricate web of lightning illuminated the park. The rows of mobile homes loomed square and still and pale against the night, reminding Nudger of tombs with awnings and TV antennas. He hadn't been back long from a trip to New Orleans, where, because of the swampy soil, the dead are interred aboveground. That was how the trailer park seemed at that moment in the storm, with no sign of anyone outside the mobile homes. Only here the dead had cars parked nearby, and occasionally one of the entombed could be seen moving behind a draped window.

Nudger shivered, and held his black umbrella at a sharp angle against the wind as he walked. He slipped a hand into his pocket and pulled out a scrap of paper. Squinting fiercely, tilting his head to the side to catch faint light off the paper, he double-checked the address he was trying to find in the maze of trailers. Though the night was warm, the rain was oddly cold and seemed to find its way down the back of his neck no matter how he held his umbrella. He stuffed the water-spotted paper back into his pocket and walked on, trailing a wing-tip shoe through a deep puddle and cursing softly.

Finally, at the end of Tranquillity Lane, he found number 307 and knocked on its metal door.

He didn't have long to wait. There was a light on inside the trailer; he saw someone's shadow cross a drawn shade, moving toward the door. The wind shot some more rain his way and threatened to snatch the umbrella away from him and play roughly with it. He felt the wet plastic handle rotate powerfully in his grip and squeezed it tighter, edging in closer to the trailer for shelter.

"I'm Nudger," he said, when the door opened.

For several seconds the woman in the doorway stood staring out at him, rain blowing in beneath the trailer's small metal awning to spot her cornflower-colored dress and ruffle her straw-blond hair. She was tall but very thin, fragile-looking, and appeared at first glance to be about twelve years old. Nudger's second glance revealed her to be in her mid-twenties. She had slight crow's feet at the corners of her pale blue eyes when she winced as a raindrop struck her face, a knowing cast to her oversized, full-lipped mouth with its slightly buck teeth. There was no one who could look much like her, no middle ground with her; men would consider her scrawny and homely, or they would see her as uniquely sensuous. Nudger liked coltish girl-women; he catalogued her as attractive.

"Whoee!" she said at last, as if seeing Nudger for the first time as she'd stepped out to check the weather. "Ain't it raining something terrible?"

"It is," Nudger agreed. "And on me."

Her entire thin body gave a quick, nervous kind of jerk as she smiled apologetically. "I'm Candy Ann Adams, Mr. Nudger. And you are getting wet, all right. Come on in."

She moved aside and Nudger stepped up into the trailer. He expected it to be surprisingly spacious; he'd once lived in and had his office in a trailer and remembered it as such. But this one was cramped and confining. The furniture was cheap and its upholstery threadbare. A portable black-and-white TV on a tiny table near the Scotch-plaid sofa was blaring shouts of ecstasy emitted by "Let's Make a Deal" contestants. It was hot in here, and the air was thick with the smell of something greasy that had been fried too long.

Candy Ann cleared a stack of *People* magazines from a vinyl chair and motioned with a lissome arm for Nudger to sit down. He folded his umbrella, left it leaning by the door, and sat. Candy

Ann started to say something, then jerked her thin body in that peculiar way of hers, almost a twitch, as if she'd just remembered something not only with her mind but with her blood and muscle, and walked over and switched off the noisy television; a heavyset dark-haired woman with bangs screamed joyfully as she disappeared from the screen. In the abrupt silence, the rain seemed to beat on the metal roof with inspired fury. Maybe the storm was a Monty Hall fan.

"That's some quieter, so we can talk," Candy Ann proclaimed, sitting opposite Nudger on the undersized sofa. Her voice had a soft Ozark lilt to it, not unpleasant. "You a sure-enough private investigator?"

"I'm that," Nudger said. "Did someone recommend me to you, Miss Adams?"

"Gotcha out of the Yellow Pages. And if you're gonna work for me, it might as well be Candy Ann without the Adams."

"Except on the check," Nudger said.

She grinned a devilish twelve-year-old's grin. "Oh, sure, don't worry none about that. I wrote you out a check already, just gotta fill in the amount. That is, if you agree to take the job. You might not."

"Why not?"

"It has to do with my fiancé, Curtis Colt."

Nudger listened for a few seconds to the rain crashing on the roof. The name Curtis Colt rattled around with familiarity in his mind, and with an unsettling connotation. It didn't take him long to place where he'd heard it, read it. All over the news media a year or so ago, and again more recently. He said, "The Curtis Colt who's going to be executed next week?"

"That's the one. Only he didn't kill that liquor-store woman. I know it for a fact, Mr. Nudger. It ain't right he should have to ride the lightning."

"'Ride the lightning'?"

"That's what convicts call dying in the electric chair, Mr.

Nudger." She crossed her thin bare arms, cupping her elbows in her hands, as if she were cold. "They call that chair lotsa things: Old Sparky . . . The Hot Squat . . . The Lord's Frying Pan. But Curtis don't belong sitting in it wired up, and I can prove it."

"It's a little late for that kind of talk," Nudger said. "Or did you testify for Curtis in court?"

"Nope. Couldn't testify. You'll see why. All them lawyers and the judge and jury don't even know about me. Curtis didn't want them to know, so he never told them." Keeping her grip-locked arms drawn in close to her body, she crossed her legs and swung her left calf jauntily; the arms and legs might have belonged to two different people conveying two different moods. Her face went with the legs; she was smiling as if trying to flirt him into wanting to know more about the job, so he could free Curtis Colt by a governor's reprieve at the last minute, just like in an old movie. Was Curtis Colt even now talking out of the corner of his mouth about tunneling under a wall?

Nudger studied her gauntly pretty, country-girl face and said, "Tell me about Curtis Colt."

"You mean you didn't read about him in the newspapers or see him on the television?"

"I only scan the media for misinformation. Give me the details."

"Well, they say Curtis was inside the liquor store, sticking it up—him and his partner had done three other places that night, all of 'em gas stations, though—when this old man that owned the place came out of a back room and seen his wife with her hands up and Curtis holding the gun on her. So the old man lost his head and ran at Curtis, and Curtis had to shoot him. He had no choice whatsoever. Then the woman got mad when she seen that and ran at Curtis, and Curtis shot her. She's the one that died. The old man, he'll live, but he can't talk nor think nor even feed himself."

Nudger remembered more about the case now. Curtis Colt had been found guilty of first-degree murder, and because of the debate in the legislature over the merits of cyanide gas versus electricity, the state was breaking out the electric chair to make him the first killer executed in Missouri by electricity in over a quarter of a century. Those of the back-to-basics school considered that progress.

"They're gonna shoot Curtis full of electricity next Saturday, Mr. Nudger," Candy Ann said plaintively. She sounded like a little girl complaining that the grade on her report card wasn't fair.

"I know," Nudger said. "But I don't see how I can help you. Or, more specifically, help Curtis Colt."

"You know what they say thoughts really are, Mr. Nudger?" Candy Ann said, ignoring his professed helplessness. Her wide blue eyes were vague as she searched for words. "Thoughts ain't nothing but tiny electrical impulses in the brain. I read that somewheres or other. What I can't help wondering is, when they shoot all that electricity into Curtis, what's it gonna be like to his thinking? How long will it seem like to him before he finally dies? Will there by a big burst of crazy thoughts along with the pain? I know it sounds loony, but I can't help laying awake nights thinking about that, and I feel I just gotta do whatever's left to try and help Curtis."

There was a sort of checkout-line-tabloid logic in that, Nudger conceded; if thoughts were actually weak electrical impulses, then high-voltage electrical impulses could become exaggerated, horrible thoughts. Anyway, try to disprove it to Candy Ann, who whiled away her time with *People* and game shows.

"They never did catch Curtis' buddy, the driver who sped away and left him in that service station, did they?" Nudger asked.

"Nope. Curtis never told who the driver was, neither, no matter how much he was threatened. Curtis is a stubborn man."

Nudger was getting the idea. "But you know who was driving the car."

"Yep. And he told me him and Curtis was miles away from that liquor store at the time it was robbed. When he seen the police closing in on Curtis at that gas station where Curtis was buying cigarettes, he hit the accelerator and got out of the parking lot before they could catch him. The police didn't even get the car's license-plate number."

Nudger rubbed a hand across his chin, watching Candy Ann swing her leg as if it were a shapely metronome. She was barefoot and wearing no nylon hose. "The jury thought Curtis not only was at the liquor store, but that he shot the old man and woman in cold blood."

"That purely ain't true, though. Not according to—" She caught herself before uttering the man's name.

"Curtis' friend," Nudger finished.

"That's right. And he oughta know," Candy Ann said righteously. The rain took another whack at the trailer; something metal moaned in the wind. The trailer rocked, caught in a Missouri summertime monsoon. All this rain was good for the farmers, the ones who still had farms.

"None of this means anything unless the driver comes forward and substantiates that he was with Curtis somewhere other than at the liquor store when it was robbed."

Candy Ann nodded and stopped swinging her leg. "I know. But he won't. He can't. That's where you come in."

"My profession might enjoy a reputation a notch lower than dognapper," Nudger said, "but I don't hire out to do anything illegal."

"What I want you to do is legal," Candy Ann said in a hurt little voice. Nudger looked past her into the dollhouse kitchen and saw an empty gin bottle on the sink counter. He wondered if she might be slightly sloshed. "It's the eyewitness accounts that got Curtis convicted," she went on. "And those people are mixed up. I want you to figure out some way to convince them it wasn't Curtis they seen that night."

"Correct me if I'm wrong, but four people, two of them customers in the liquor store, picked Curtis out of a police lineup."

"You ain't wrong. But so what if them four did identify Curtis? Who thinks or sees straight when there's a shooting going on? Ain't eyewitnesses often mistaken?"

Nudger had to admit that they were, though he didn't see how they could be in this case. There were, after all, four of them. And yet, Candy Ann was right; it was amazing how people could sometimes be so certain that the wrong man had committed a crime just five feet in front of them.

"I want you to talk to them witnesses," Candy Ann said. "Find out *why* they think Curtis was the killer. Then show them how they might be wrong and get them to change what they said."

"That might be like throwing chaff into the wind," Nudger said, "to put it politely."

"Except we got the truth on our side, Mr. Nudger. At least one witness will change his story when he's made to think about it. Because Curtis wasn't where they said he was. He was someplace else, and that's a fact as solid and unchangeable as the sun and the stars."

"The sun and stars are expanding," Nudger told her. "Flying apart at millions of miles per hour. The Big Bang theory, scientists call it."

"I wouldn't know nothing about some big bang, Mr. Nudger. What I know is that Curtis didn't kill nobody."

"Curtis has exhausted all his appeals," Nudger said to this hopelessly naive girl-woman. "Even if all the witnesses changed their stories, it wouldn't necessarily mean he'd get a new trial."

"Maybe not, but I betcha they wouldn't kill him. They couldn't stand the publicity if enough witnesses said they was wrong, it was somebody else shot the old woman. Then, just maybe, eventually, Curtis would get another trial and get out of prison."

Nudger stared at her. He was awed. Here was foolish optimism that transcended even his own. He had to admire Candy Ann.

The shapely pale leg started pumping again beneath the cornflower-blue dress. When Nudger lowered his gaze to stare at it, Candy Ann said, "So will you help me, Mr. Nudger?"

"Sure," Nudger said. "It sounds easy."

2

Nudger sat on his customary red vinyl stool at the end of the stainless-steel counter in Danny's Donuts, staring at the stack of glossy copies of newspaper pages before him. He'd spent the morning in the county library out on Lindbergh, poring over old news stories about Curtis Colt and copying the pages he thought were pertinent. He felt slightly nauseated. Sitting and staring at one of those library microfilm viewers while blown up pictures of newspaper pages rolled past was something like sitting by a window in a moving train; it gave Nudger the same sensation as motion sickness.

He'd felt better by the time he got to his office, which was located on the second floor, directly above the doughnut shop. So he decided to come down here, talk with Danny, and have a Dunker Delite and a glass of milk for lunch. But doleful Danny was out of milk, and apologized profusely and pressed on Nudger a free bottomless cup of coffee to go with his free Dunker Delite. Nudger's stomach was queasy again within minutes. The Dunker Delite was tolerable. The coffee, which Danny solicitously kept at rim level in its foam cup, was at its worst. Which was like saying Son of Sam was in a nasty mood.

"What's all that stuff about?" Danny asked Nudger, when the last of his few afternoon customers had left the shop.

"Curtis Colt," Nudger said.

Danny read the papers daily and was something of a crime buff. "The guy Governor Scalla wants to fry instead of send out with gas?"

"The same," Nudger said, gazing at his Dunker Delite. Scott Scalla was a hard-nosed former attorney general who had been elected mainly due to his pledge to implement capital punishment, and who favored the electric chair over the gas chamber. Most of the legislature in Jefferson City, the state capital, opted for using the gas chamber if Missouri had to begin executing convicted killers again. Sly politician that he was, Scalla had used the argument over *how* for the purpose of diverting attention from the argument over *if*. Curtis Colt was either going to inhale cyanide gas or he was going to ride the lightning. The *if* question had been settled just before Colt was tagged for the electric chair.

"How come you need to learn about Colt?" Danny asked, wiping down the smooth counter and tucking his grayish towel back into his belt. "After Saturday, not much of what you know about him will matter anymore. He'll be gone."

"Probably," Nudger said. He pretended to sip his coffee while Danny watched with his sad brown eyes. "You think he's guilty of killing that woman, Danny?"

"Sure. He was found guilty by twelve good men and true."

"There were eight women on the jury," Nudger pointed out.

"Sex aside," Danny said, pausing for a moment to remove the towel from his belt and snap it at a bluebottle fly that had settled on the counter, "Colt is guilty. The truth comes out in court."

"It does," Nudger agreed, watching the fly buzz frantically away through a shaft of gold sunlight, spiraling up, up, winging for life. Beautiful. "But sometimes not all of the truth. And not in any form you might recognize."

"It don't matter much now," Danny said. "What's done's done. The law says Colt did it, and he's only got a week to live. So what are you doing digging around in the case, Nudge?"

"I was hired by somebody who thinks Colt's innocent."

"Humph," Danny said, and bent down to rearrange the leftover cream horns in the greasy display case. One of the spread-out newspapers on which he'd placed waxed paper in the case was today's sports page. "The Cards have won four in a row now," he said, reading beyond the cream horns. "We get some relief pitching and we'll take the division championship."

Nudger wished there were a relief corps for every occupation; there were a lot of times he could have used a relief detective. He slid his coffee cup off to the side and got back to reading.

The papers agreed on the details of the crime. Two customers in the back of the liquor store heard shots, looked down the aisle, and saw Curtis Colt standing over the body of the old man who owned and managed the store. Colt was holding a gun. The man's wife, also shot, was staggering around the store, grabbing on to things and knocking over displays and bottles. Colt shoved her aside and ran.

Two witnesses outside saw him, still holding the gun, race from the store and get into a parked car whose driver was waiting with the engine idling. One of the witnesses, a Mrs. Langeneckert, screamed for him to stop. Another shot was fired wildly as the car sped away.

The liquor-store owner, sixty-eight-year-old Amos Olson, had been shot once in the head and twice in the abdomen. One of the bullets had tumbled and damaged his spine and central nervous system. He would never give his version of the crime. He would never talk or perhaps even think coherently again.

Olson's wife Dolly, same age as her husband, had been hit only once, but with deadly accuracy in the forehead. Nudger knew that the forehead was one of the least effective places to shoot a human being; unlike the back of the skull, there was a great deal of bone there to protect the brain. Sometimes people shot in the forehead took a long time to die. Which was why Dolly Olson had thrashed about the store for a while in a blind frenzy before mercifully dropping dead.

The Dunker Delite seemed to shift weighty position in Nudger's stomach, as if it couldn't get comfortable and wished it were someplace else. His large intestine told him he had too much imagination. He swallowed noisily and read on.

An hour later that evening, a cruising two-man patrol car had stopped at a service station so one of the police officers could use the rest room. As they pulled up by the pumps, a black or dark green car, probably a Ford, screeched from a shadowed corner of the lot. The cruiser's engine was turned off, and as the driver tried to start the car his partner spotted someone standing by the cigarette machine inside the station. The someone looked terrified and matched the description of the liquor-store woman's killer that had recently been broadcast on the police radio. The car that had sped from the lot matched the general description of the liquor-store-holdup getaway car.

The cop forgot all about using the rest room.

Half an hour later, Colt was handcuffed and booked at the Third District station house. The black or dark green Ford and its driver weren't seen again.

It was exactly the kind of case a prosecuting attorney prayed for. The jury was out less than an hour before finding Colt guilty. Colt had shot the old man first; he'd had time to think about killing the woman. He could simply have run from the liquor store, but he hadn't. He'd stayed. Premeditation of a sort. The judge recommended the death penalty. The jury went along with that one, too. Everybody was ripe for somebody else's death.

Nudger studied the photographs of Colt, trying to get a feel for who and what the man was. On the front page of the *Post-Dispatch* was a shot of Colt being led into the Third District station. In the next day's paper there was a close up of him, handsome in a moody, defiant way, with lean, dark features that looked as if they'd been whittled from hard wood. He was young, with a downswept bandito mustache and wavy dark hair that fell gracefully over his ears and collar. Another shot of him, being led from police headquarters at Tucker and Clark, showed him considerably calmer than on the night of his arrest. He was wearing jail-house dungarees and his wrists were cuffed in front of him. He was somewhat on the short side, compared with the two detectives flanking him in the photo, and had a skinny middleweight's lithe and muscular build.

"What are you supposed to be able to do for this guy?" Danny was asking.

"Save his life," Nudger said, folding his newspaper copies and placing the coffee cup directly before him.

Danny was staring at the cup, whose level hadn't dropped much in the last fifteen minutes. He was almost as sensitive about his coffee as about his doughnuts, which were not quite as lethal.

Nudger had no choice; hurting Danny's feelings was like kicking a tired old basset hound. He poured more cream into the coffee, loaded in two heaping spoonfuls of sugar to cut the bitterness, and took a sip. Not bad. Well, not fatal. He looked over at Danny and smiled.

Danny smiled back and went to the big steel coffee urn and adjusted some valves; something toward the back of the urn hissed and emitted steam. He looked like a submariner getting ready to send his craft on a crash dive into protective depths, where it would lie on the bottom, weighted down with Dunker Delites. "Scalla ain't the sort to give reprieves," he said over his shoulder.

"I know. He's the type to throw the switch himself."

"I don't know what just reminded me," Danny said, "but Eileen was by here this morning looking for you. She seemed eager for you and her to be in the same place at the same time."

Nudger's stomach kicked. Hard. Eileen was his former wife. Since the divorce, she and his stomach got along worse every year. "She say what she wanted?"

"Not directly," Danny said, "but she hinted it was green and you owed it to her."

"Not this time," Nudger said. "I'm caught up on my alimony."

As he spoke, Nudger suddenly wondered if that was true. Had his last check to her been for half the amount owed? Had there been enough money in the account to cover the check? It was all misty memory.

Danny shrugged and wiped his hands roughly on the towel, in the manner of a mechanic who'd just crawled out from under a car and was uncertain about his work. "Well, I dunno, Nudge. You want another doughnut?"

"No, thanks. Work to do." Nudger swiveled away from the counter and slid down off his stool. He picked up his foam coffee cup and headed for the door.

"You really think Colt might be innocent?" Danny asked. He sounded dubious.

"I never said that," Nudger told him.

He pushed out through the door into the hot day, made a tight U-turn, and went in the door to the narrow, creaking stairway that led up to his office. The sweet smell of the doughnut shop followed him.

After switching on the window air conditioner, he sat in his squealing swivel chair behind his desk and checked his telephone answering machine. There was a click, whir, and a beep, and the first message sounded.

A drunk, almost unintelligible, painstakingly explained that he'd called the wrong number and asked for the right one. He got angry when no one accepted his apology, and hung up in a snit.

Beep. Eileen's voice: "Call me today, if you know what's good for you. If you don't—"

Nudger punched the machine's off button. He didn't know what was good for him. Never had.

He sat back in his chair. He'd heard enough messages for now, and the mail he'd brought in from the landing didn't look interesting: bills, ads, threatening letters from creditors, bills, junk mail, bills, bills. He made up his mind not to open any of the mail until he needed something to do.

The office was getting comfortably cool. It didn't take long; the place was small. Nudger watched the electric bill on the desk flutter lazily in the breeze from the air conditioner. Finally it slid off the desk and sailed toward the far wall, out of sight. He didn't bother to retrieve it.

He went through the Curtis Colt information again, this time more carefully, and decided Colt was guilty as original sin.

Nudger didn't like where that left him.

He'd have liked it even less if he'd known where it was taking him.

3

Nudger looked at the list of names he'd compiled and decided to start with Randy Gantner. Gantner and a friend had been in the liquor store at the time of the shooting and had testified for the prosecution in court. He was as good a place as any to begin—the logical place, really, since it occurred to Nudger that there were so many witnesses against Curtis Colt that he might as well talk to them in alphabetical order.

Randy Gantner was a construction worker for Kalas Construction, one of the major contractors in St. Louis, a road builder who did a lot of highway work. Nudger had seen the company name lettered across truck trailers parked at major road construction sites all over the city. Road contractors not only did this to advertise; the countless permits they needed to work were plastered all over the sides of the trailers to satisfy various inspectors and busybody local officials.

It was afternoon before Nudger located Gantner working weekend overtime on a highway access ramp job in Northwest County. Kalas Construction was building a new cloverleaf on the stem of Interstate 70. It was hot work and a hot afternoon to do it in.

"Why should I worry about it anymore?" Gantner asked Nudger, leaning hipshot on his shovel. He didn't mind talking to Nudger; it meant taking a break from scooping away mounds of black dirt that had been brought up by a huge drill that was boring holes to bedrock for concrete piering. "Colt's been found guilty and he's going to the chair, ain't he?"

The high afternoon sun was hammering down on Nudger, warming the back of his neck and making his stomach uneasy. He thumbed an antacid tablet off the roll he kept in his shirt pocket and popped one of the white disks into his mouth. With his other hand he held up a photograph of Curtis Colt for Gantner to see. It was a snapshot Candy Ann had given him of the wiry, shirtless Colt leaning on a crooked fence post with a placid lake behind him and holding a beer can high in a mock toast: This one's for Death!

Why am I doing this? Nudger asked himself. It was hopeless. He could *feel* Colt's guilt. The jury had been right.

But he said, "This is a photograph you never saw in court. I just want you to look at it closely and tell me again if you're sure the man you saw in the liquor store was Colt. Even if it makes no difference in whether he's executed, it will help ease the mind of someone who loves him."

Gantner was a ruddy, beefy man, shirtless in the sun. A rivulet of sweat zigzagged like an exploring insect down through the gingery hair on his chest. He shifted his weight against the shovel handle to lean with his other arm. "I'd be a fool to change my story about what happened now that the trial's over," he said logically.

"You'd be a murderer if you really weren't sure."

"The little punk's gonna fry; I don't see the point in this."

"There's a point," Nudger assured him.

Gantner sighed, dragged a dirty red handkerchief from his jeans pocket, and wiped his meaty, perspiring face. He peered at the photo with pale eyes framed in seamed, tan flesh, then shrugged. "It's him. Colt. The guy I seen shoot the man and woman when I was standing in the back aisle of the liquor store. If he'd known me and Sanders was back there, he'd have probably zapped us along with them old folks. He was having a hell of a good time playing Jesse James. Little fart richly deserves to get the chair, you ask me."

Well, Nudger *had* asked. But he wanted to make doubly sure. "You're positive it's the same man?"

Gantner spat off to the side and frowned; Nudger was becoming a pest, and the foreman was staring. "I said it to the police and the jury, Nudger, and now I'm saying it to you: Colt did the old lady in."

Persistent Nudger. "Did you actually see the shots fired?"

"Nope. Me and Sanders was in the back aisle looking for some reasonable-priced bourbon when we heard the shots, then looked around to the front of the store. There was Colt, standing over the old man, holding a gun. Then the old lady sees what happened and screams and runs out from behind the counter at Colt, at the gun. Give her top grades for guts. Colt holds the gun higher and shoots her. She goes wild and starts twitching and bouncing all over the place, knocking good whiskey all to hell, and Colt runs out the door to a car. Looked like a black or dark green old Ford. Colt fired another shot as it drove away."

"You try to help the old lady?"

"Sure. But by the time me and Sanders got to the front of the store, she'd gone down and we could see she was dead. Round hole smack in the center of her forehead, eyes open."

Gantner was rolling now. He knew this part of his story almost by rote from his interviews with the law and his testimony on the stand. He enjoyed telling it, polishing his delivery; show-biz was in his blood.

"Get a look at the car's driver?" Nudger asked, thumbing another antacid tablet off the roll. God, the sun was hot!

"Sort of. Skinny dude, curly black hair and a droopy mustache.

Leaning over the steering wheel and holding it tight. That's what I told the cops. That's all I seen. That's all I know."

"Where was your friend Sanders when Colt ran out the door?"

"I don't know, exactly. Around where I was, I guess. I told you, that's all I know. Finish." Gantner raised a dirt-streaked hand and traced neat printing in the air. He said with perfect enunciation, "The fucking end."

And that was the way to describe this conversation. The foreman was walking toward them, glaring. He was a big guy who swaggered like a sailor on a rolling deck. He had a hell of a glare. *Thunk!* Gantner's shovel sliced deep into the earth, speeding the day when there'd be another place for traffic to get backed up. Nudger thanked him and advised him not to work too hard in the hot sun.

"You wanna help?" Gantner asked, grinning sweatily.

"I'm already doing some digging of my own," Nudger said, walking away before the ominous foreman arrived.

He sat for a while in his dented Volkswagen Beetle with the windows rolled down. There was a faint breeze wafting through the car; it felt cool on the right side of Nudger's sweat-plastered shirt. He watched the foreman motion toward the Volkswagen, talk for a few minutes with Gantner, then walk away. Gantner kept digging, not glancing over at Nudger, as if not looking at him meant he wasn't there.

Nudger got out his spiral notebook and jotted down the pertinent parts of his conversation with Gantner. Some kind of huge machine that hammered concrete into dust rolled onto the scene then and began smashing its way noisily up the old exit ramp, like some creature from a sixties Japanese horror flick: *Crushzilla the Destroyer*. The ground trembled. Nudger wanted to stay and watch, but he had miles to go and promises to keep.

Before the state kept its promise to Curtis Colt.

The next witness Nudger talked to also stood by her identification. She was an elderly moon-faced woman with extraordinarily large watery brown eyes—Iris Langeneckert, who had been walking her dog near the liquor store and had seen Curtis Colt dash out the door and into the getaway car.

That was how she told it, simply, briefly, and with a matter-of-factness that would have swayed any jury, there in her meticulously neat south St. Louis apartment on Tennessee Avenue. Then she offered Nudger a sandwich and glass of iced tea.

Nudger declined the sandwich but accepted the tea with gratitude. It was strong, and sweet with natural sugar that still swirled gently in it from stirring and settled hazily on the bottom of the glass as pale sediment. As Nudger drank, the brown mongrel that had also witnessed the robbery-murder lay mostly concealed behind the sofa and watched him warily from half-closed eyes.

When Nudger was almost finished with the tea, Iris Langeneckert said something that Gantner had also touched on. "He was a skinny young man with curly black hair and a beard or mustache," she said, describing the getaway-car driver. Then she added, "Like Curtis Colt's hair and mustache."

Nudger looked again at the lakeside snapshot Candy Ann had given him. There was Curtis Colt, about five feet nine, skinny, and handsomely mean-looking with that broad bandito mustache and mop of curly, greasy black hair. There was a don't-give-a-damnness even in the way he stood, legs spread a little too wide, shoulders set as if to punch first if anyone even drew back a hand to threaten to strike him. A chin that proclaimed he could take it, cold eyes that said he could dish it out. Nudger had seen a lot like him. Too many. They were so alike, part of the world's pattern of pain and desperation. He wondered if it was possible that the getaway-car driver had been Colt himself, and his accomplice had killed the old woman. Even Nudger found that one difficult to believe.

He thanked Mrs. Langeneckert, then drove to his office in the near-suburb of Maplewood and sat behind his desk in the blast of cold air from the window unit, sipping the complimentary cup of diet cola he'd brought up from Danny's Donuts. The smell of the doughnut shop was heavier than usual in the office; maybe something to do with the heat and humidity. Nudger had never quite gotten used to the cloying sugar-grease scent and what it did to his sensitive stomach.

When he was cool enough to think clearly again, he decided he needed additional information on the holdup, and on Curtis Colt, from a more objective source than Candy Ann Adams. He phoned Police Lieutenant Jack Hammersmith at home and was told by Hammersmith's son Jed that Hammersmith had just driven away and it would be late before he returned.

Nudger checked his answering machine again, proving that hope did indeed spring eternal in a fool's breast.

There was another terse message from Eileen, telling him to call her but not saying what about; a solemn-voiced young man reading an address where Nudger could send a check to help pay to form a watchdog committee that would stop the utilities from continually raising their rates; and a cheerful man informing Nudger that with the labels from ten packages of a brand-name hot dog he could get a Cardinals ballgame ticket at half price. (That meant eating over eighty hot dogs. Nudger calculated that baseball season would be over by the time he did that.) Everyone seemed to want some of Nudger's money. No one wanted to pay Nudger any money. Except for Candy Ann Adams. Nudger decided he'd better shrug off some of his pessimism and step up his efforts on the Curtis Colt case.

He tilted back his head, drained the last dribble of cola, then tried to eat what was left of the crushed ice. But the ice clung stubbornly to the bottom of the cup, taunting him. Nudger's life was like that.

He crumpled the paper cup and lobbed it, ice and all, into the wastebasket.

4

The next morning Police Lieutenant Jack Hammersmith was in his Third District office, obese, sleek, and cool-looking behind his wide metal desk. There was a comfortable grace to his corpulence, like that of a seal under water. He was pounds and years away from the handsome cop who'd been Nudger's partner a decade ago in a two-man patrol car. Nudger could still see traces of a dashing quality in the flesh-upholstered Hammersmith, but he wondered if that was only because he'd known him ten years ago.

"Sit down, Nudge," Hammersmith invited, his lips smiling but his grayish-blue cop's eyes unreadable. If eyes were the windows to the soul, his shades were always down.

Nudger sat in one of the straight-backed chairs in front of Hammersmith's desk. The desk was neat: a phone, brown plastic "in" and "out" baskets, two stacks of papers, some file folders, a glass ashtray with a chip out of it, all of it symmetrically arranged. Hammersmith was always busy, always organized, always—well, sometimes—ready to assist his old strayed-away sidekick.

"I need some help," Nudger said.

"Sure," Hammersmith said, "you never come see me just to trade recipes or to sit and rock." Hammersmith was partial to irony; it was a good thing in his line of work. Nudger thought it might be what kept him sane.

"I need to know more about Curtis Colt," Nudger told him.

Hammersmith got one of his vile greenish cigars out of his shirt pocket and stared intently at it, as if its paper-ring label might reveal some secret of life and death. "Colt, eh? The guy who's going to ride the lightning?"

"That's the second time in the past few days I've heard that expression. The first time was from Colt's fiancée. She thinks he's innocent."

"Fiancées think along those lines. Is she your client, this woman who's already picked one loser?"

Nudger nodded, but didn't volunteer Candy Ann's name.

"Gullibility makes the world go round," Hammersmith said. "I was in charge of that one. There's not a chance Colt is innocent, Nudge."

"Four eyewitness IDs are compelling evidence," Nudger admitted.

"Damning evidence," Hammersmith said.

"What about the getaway-car driver? His description is a lot like Colt's. Maybe he's the one who did the shooting and Colt was the driver."

"Colt's lawyer hit on that. The jury didn't buy it. Neither do I. The man is guilty, Nudge."

"You know how inaccurate eyewitness accounts are," Nudger persisted.

That seemed to get Hammersmith mad. He lit the cigar. The office immediately fogged up. Even considering their hugeness, Hammersmith's cigars generated a tremendous amount of smoke in proportion to their size. And they burned fast, like fuses; sometimes their coarse tobacco even made a faint crackling sound. Yet they never seemed to burn down to butt size so they mercifully could be extinguished.

Nudger made his tone more amicable. "Mind if I look at the file on the Colt case?"

Hammersmith gazed thoughtfully at Nudger through a dense greenish haze. He inhaled, exhaled; the haze became a cloud. "How come this fiancée didn't turn up at the trial to testify for Colt? She could have at least lied and said he was with her locked in steamy sex that night. Hell, that's traditional."

The smoke was beginning to affect Nudger's stomach violently; he felt as if he ought to swallow, but he didn't allow it to happen.

It made talking difficult. "Colt apparently didn't want her subjected to taking the stand," he said in an odd, phlegmy voice.

"How noble," Hammersmith said. "What makes this fiancée think her Prince Charming is innocent?"

"She knows he was somewhere else when the shopkeepers were shot."

"But not with her?"

"Nope."

"Well, that's refreshing."

Maybe it was refreshing enough to make up Hammersmith's mind. He picked up the phone and asked for the Colt file. Nudger could barely make out what he was saying around the fat cigar, but apparently everyone at the Third was used to Hammersmith and could interpret cigarese.

Nudger finally allowed himself to swallow. Yuk. Beyond the hazy office window, the summer air looked clear and sweet and shimmering, beckoning in bright sunlight. St. Louis, the Sultry City, had its alluring moments.

The file, which was mostly a mishmash of fan-fold computer paper, didn't reveal much that Nudger didn't know. Same account of the crime as was in the newspapers. Same eyewitness testimony, almost word for word. Twenty minutes after the liquor-store shooting, Colt was interrupted by officers Wayne Callister and Elvis Jefferson while buying cigarettes from a vending machine at a service station on Hanley Road. A car that had been parked near the end of the dimly lighted lot had sped away before they'd entered the station's office. Both Callister and Jefferson had gotten only a glimpse of a black or dark green old Ford; they hadn't made out the license-plate number, but Callister thought it started with the letter *L*.

Colt had surrendered without a struggle, and that night at the Third District station the four eyeball witnesses had picked him out of a lineup. Their description of the getaway car matched that of the car the police had seen speeding from the service station. The loot from the holdup, and several gas-station holdups committed earlier that night, wasn't on Colt, but it was probably in the car. A paraffin test on Colt's hands turned up nitrate traces, indicating that he'd recently fired a weapon.

"Colt's innocence just jumps out of the file at you, doesn't it, Nudge?" Hammersmith said. He was grinning a fat grin around the fat cigar.

"Paraffin tests aren't foolproof," Nudger said. But he knew they were virtually always right; Colt had fired a gun.

"They aren't even admissible in court," Hammersmith said. "The evidence against Colt was so strong, that didn't make any difference."

"What about the murder weapon?"

"Colt was unarmed when we picked him up."

"Seems odd."

"Not really," Hammersmith said. "He was planning to pay for the cigarettes. And maybe the gun was still too hot to touch, so he left it in the car. Maybe it's still hot; it got a lot of use for one night."

Closing the file folder and laying it on a corner of Hammersmith's desk, Nudger stood up. He was relieved to find that the air was more breathable in the upper half of the room. "Thanks, Jack. I'll keep you tapped in if I learn anything interesting."

Hammersmith waved the cigar gracefully, almost as if conducting a silent orchestra. "Don't bother keeping me informed on this one, Nudge. It's over. I don't see how even a fiancée can doubt Colt's guilt."

Nudger shrugged, trying not to breathe too deeply in the smoke-hazed office. "Maybe it's an emotional thing. She thinks that because thought waves are tiny electrical impulses, Colt might experience time warp and all sorts of grotesque thoughts when all that voltage shoots through him. She thinks he might die a long and horrible death. She has bad dreams."

"I'll bet she does," Hammersmith said. "I'll bet Colt has bad dreams, too. Only he deserves his."

"Is there any doubt the switch is going to be thrown?" Nudger asked.

Hammersmith bit down on his cigar and shook his head. "No doubt at all. This one is Governor Scalla's personal project. Once Colt became a convicted felon and ceased to be a voter, all hope was lost."

Though he believed in the necessity of capital punishment, Hammersmith was no fan of Governor Scott Scalla. Hammersmith was a good man and a good cop; he didn't like the methods Scalla had used to put people away when the governor was attorney general.

Early in Scalla's career, he'd seen to it that all the juveniles he'd tried received maximum sentences when convicted; he'd often done this by plea-bargaining and letting their confederates serve lighter terms in exchange for their cooperation and a sure conviction. As long as those terms kept the juveniles in prison until they were twenty-one, it was all fine with Scalla. That way he could brag about juvenile crime statistics decreasing under his special attention, not mentioning that these juveniles were often back out on the streets adding to adult crime statistics. Crime paid for Scalla; it had helped to get him elected governor despite the often-accurate charges by his opponent that he had used his office of state attorney mainly to further his political career, and that he had been bought and was controlled by several special-interest groups.

Scalla blithely denied all of these charges, all the while decrying the evils of crime and espousing the biblical credo of eye-for-an-eye. He belonged to a stiff-backed religion, something called Friends of God, occasionally played piano and sang gospel music, smiled boyishly and often, and had a wife who wore no lipstick. How could you not believe a guy like that?

"Maybe the fiancée is right," Hammersmith said.

"About what?"

"About all that voltage distorting thought and time. Who's to say?"

"Not Curtis Colt," Nudger said. "Not after they throw the switch."

"It's a nice theory, though," Hammersmith said. "I'll remember it. It might be a comforting thing to tell the murder victim's family."

"Sometimes," Nudger said, "you think just like a cop who's seen too much."

"Any of it's too much, Nudge," Hammersmith said with surprising sadness. He let more greenish smoke drift from his nostrils and the corners of his mouth; he looked like a stone Buddha seated behind the desk, one in which incense burned.

Nudger coughed and said good-bye. His eyes stung and watered for twenty minutes after he got outside.

5

After leaving Hammersmith, Nudger located and phoned Gantner's drinking buddy, Roy Sanders, at a tire-retreading plant out in Westport where Sanders worked. Sanders was working overtime, as Gantner had been yesterday. Busy, busy. Industry was thriving. Sanders agreed to talk with Nudger during his lunch break, which was in about fifteen minutes.

Nudger got to Westport, a business and warehouse complex in West County, in twenty minutes, and found Sanders sitting with four other men in the employee's lounge of Roll-On Recap City.

The lounge was a long, narrow room, painted workplace green and lined with colorful vending machines that seemed to sell

everything from sandwiches to birth-control devices. There were a
lot of potted plants suspended from the ceiling in front of the window at the far end, spilling lush viny greenness almost to the floor.
On the windowsill sat opened boxes of plant food and a mist-
sprayer.

Sanders, a tall, Lincolnesque man with dark smudges on his
bare arms, carefully placed his cheese sandwich on a white paper
napkin and shook hands with Nudger. Everyone at the table was
dressed in a workshirt and dark-stained jeans and was wearing a
similarly soiled blue work apron. Picking up his coffee and sandwich, Sanders led Nudger to a table near the end of the long room,
where they could talk privately.

"You want a cup of coffee?" he asked Nudger, before they sat
down at the gray Formica table.

Nudger said no thanks, and they sat. Neither man said anything
while a tall, redheaded woman in a business suit stalked into the
lounge, deposited coins in a soup machine near the table, then
cursed mightily because the machine hadn't freed the little captive
soup can from its glass cell but had kept the proffered ransom. The
woman kicked the machine softly but precisely with the pointed
toe of a high-heeled shoe, as if aiming for its groin, before moving
down the lounge to another bank of machines that might prove
more amiable.

Nudger went through the routine he'd pursued with Gantner.
The answers were the same. Sanders and Gantner had been in the
rear of the store, heard shots, saw the old man on the floor, the old
woman staggering around with a bullet wound in her head. Saw
her fall, saw Curtis Colt run from the store, gun in hand, and get
into a dark green car that screeched away. Sanders had only caught
a glimpse of the car as it sped past the display window, and said he
didn't hear the shot Colt had allegedly fired from the speeding car.

"Did you get a good look at Colt's face?" Nudger asked, knowing Sanders had testified in court that he had.

Sanders took a big bite of his cheese sandwich, chewing with his mouth open. His melancholy eyes were thoughtful. "Pretty good." For a moment Nudger thought he was commenting on the sandwich, then realized Sanders was talking about the look he'd gotten at Colt. "All this takes a lot of time to tell, but it happened fast, only a couple of seconds. I got as good a look at him as I could have in that short a time."

Nudger shoved the lakeside photo across the table for Sanders to look at again, the one where Colt was holding a beer can high in a defiant toast. "And you're sure this is the man?"

Sanders gulped coffee, wiped his mouth as he stared down at the snapshot. "I don't know that from this photo. You tell me it's Colt, I believe you. I *am* sure the man I saw in the police lineup, the guy I saw in court, was the one that was in the liquor store with the gun. The one that blasted the old guy and his wife."

"But it's the same man."

Sanders shrugged. "Hell, you know photos. You take my picture, I look handsome."

Nudger doubted that, but he nodded and put the snapshot back into his pocket. "Did you see the getaway-car driver?"

"Got a glance, is all. Guy with long darkish hair, leaning over the steering wheel like he was trying to coax more speed outa the car."

"Colt had dark hair, wavy and almost shoulder-length."

Sanders grinned. "I know where you're going with that one, Nudger. Colt's lawyer tried it in court. Tricky little bastard; I gotta give him that. Full of more twists and turns than a double-jointed break dancer. But he couldn't shake me. It was Colt I saw in that liquor store. No doubt whatsoever here. Curtis Colt."

"How do you feel about capital punishment, Mr. Sanders?"

"I believe in it. Human life's the most precious thing there is; you take somebody's and you oughta die for it. And Colt took somebody's life."

"But you didn't recognize him positively in the photograph."

"He wasn't in a photograph when he was in the liquor store."

That was a good point, Nudger conceded, looking at Sanders and thinking that with a wart on his cheek the man really would look like Lincoln.

Sanders shot a glance at his watch. "I gotta get back and grade some tires or I get docked; we're slaves here."

"I suspect someday you'll do something about that," Nudger said.

Sanders looked around furtively and lowered his voice. "You mean the union?"

"Exactly," Nudger said, and thanked him for giving up part of his lunch break and left.

As he drove from Roll-On Recap City's parking lot and turned onto Dorsett Road, Nudger realized that being in the presence of all that glassed-in food had made him hungry.

Claudia Bettencourt would be at a faculty meeting today until one o'clock. Nudger phoned her at Stowe High School and asked if she wanted to meet him for lunch. She said sure, at her apartment. Good girl.

Though he was in West County, he was still closer to Claudia's south St. Louis apartment than she was, so he got there first and let himself in with his key.

It was an old, spacious apartment on Wilmington, high-ceilinged and with steam-radiator heat. There was no central air-conditioning. The place was stuffy, with a faint scent of cooking gas mingled with the trapped summer heat. Nudger walked to the window air conditioner in the living room and switched it on. He stood for a moment in its humming, gurgling coolness, turning so the chilled draft dried his shirt where it was stuck to his back. The draperies at the opposite window caught the gentle movement of air and began swaying in slow rhythm like dreamy dance partners.

Claudia had lived in the apartment long enough for it to have taken on a settled appearance. The furniture, some of it new and financed through her job teaching at Stowe School, had adapted to its surroundings and seemed to have grown where it sat on the worn blue carpet. There was a clear glass ashtray with a compressed and bent cigarette butt in it on the coffee table and a stack of outdated newspapers on the floor alongside the sofa. Claudia didn't smoke; Nudger wondered who had snubbed out a cigarette here.

He walked into the kitchen. It was still too warm in there. He got a Budweiser out of the refrigerator, then returned to the cooler living room before popping the tab on the beer can. No need for a glass. He sat in a corner of the sofa where he could feel cool movement of air, found that morning's *Post* on top of the stack of papers, and checked the front section.

There was a photograph of Scott Scalla grinning while cutting a ribbon in front of a new factory in St. Charles. There was a piece about a county cop who had broken under strain and shot himself and his wife, and next to that a three-column article was advising people how to stay cool in the smothering grip of the present heat wave. There was nothing on Curtis Colt. He was old news and would be until a few days before his execution, when the media would get interested in whether he'd make a last-minute confession or order strawberries and pickles for his final meal. Murderers sure weren't like the rest of us; it was fun and more than a little scary to peek into their minds.

Nudger sighed, sipped beer, and turned to the sports page to read about the Cardinals' fourth straight victory. They'd won last night in extra innings. There was a photograph of Tommy Herr doing his muscular ballet over second base as he pivoted gracefully for the double play. Nudger thought Herr might be even smoother than Scott Scalla.

Claudia opened the door, pivoted neatly herself, and unloaded an armload of books and folders onto the table in the hall.

"Homework," she said, grinning at Nudger. "It's a little-known fact that teachers have more homework than their students.

All this stuff has to be graded." She was teaching summer school this year, a heavy schedule.

She looked great, wearing a simple navy-blue dress that set off her long dark hair and brown eyes. Her waist appeared especially slim in the sashed dress; her lean features were perfect except for a narrow nose that some might have found too long but that Nudger thought gave her a noble look and conveyed a subtle but volatile sexiness. Beauty was in the eye of the beholder, and Nudger liked to behold, then to hold.

He waited like a patient cobra until she got near enough, then pulled her down onto his lap and kissed her. She was heavy for her leanness, solid and strong. She returned the kiss, using her tongue.

"There are different kinds of homework," Nudger pointed out. "Some on subjects more interesting than the English you teach."

She climbed off his lap and primly straightened her dress. "It's the afternoon."

He glanced at the light streaming through the window and nodded. Afternoon, all right. A sex act might change all that, throw all the time zones out of whack.

"I've got some frozen spaghetti," she said, switching on the dining room air conditioner so it would blow into the kitchen.

Nudger knew enough to give up. For now. "That stuff in the little plastic bags you drop into boiling water?"

She didn't answer. He heard her clattering around in the kitchen. A piece of flatware hit the floor, bounced; water ran.

By the time he'd finished his beer and was done reading about the ballgame, she had two plates of spaghetti, some cloverleaf rolls, Parmesan cheese, and two glasses of red wine on the dining room table. Nudger was glad to see there was no garlic bread.

He sat down across from her at the table. "Did you see the girls this weekend?" The girls were Nora and Joan, her young daughters by her marriage to despicable Ralph Ferris.

Claudia nodded, striking viciously at the spaghetti with her fork. The Ralph effect. He wasn't surprised when she said, "I saw Ralph, too."

"How is he?"

"The same. A deceiving bastard."

Nudger was glad to hear her speak so about Ralph. She used to speak derogatorily about him only infrequently. She'd thought everything that had gone wrong with their marriage, with their children, had been her fault. Ralph had helped her to think that, helped her down into hell. Which was why Ralph was indeed a deceiving bastard.

Nudger sipped wine, smiled. Ralph was also a fool. Claudia was a woman you could talk to, but one who didn't press for answers or explanations. And Nudger seldom delved into her life where she'd made it plain she didn't want him. Such mutual respect and trust was rare in a relationship where there was good sex.

"What do you think of Curtis Colt?" Nudger said.

Claudia swallowed a mouthful of spaghetti, washed it down with Gallo wine. "The guy who shot that old couple in a supermarket holdup?"

"Liquor store," Nudger corrected. "My job is to prove he's innocent."

"I thought his legal counsel had tried taking care of all that in court, and Colt was found guilty and sentenced to death."

"That's the way it is, I'm afraid. His fiancée hired me to talk to the witnesses who testified against him, uncover enough doubt to stave off his execution in the electric chair."

"Which execution is? . . ."

"Saturday."

"Sounds as if you're tilting at a windmill. The kind that generates electricity."

"Cruel analogy, teacher."

She smiled at him as she buttered a roll. "Were you looking for encouragement?"

"Nope. Objectivity."

"That's what you got," she said. "Sorry."

When they were finished eating, he carried the dishes into the kitchen while she loaded the dishwasher. Claudia was very efficient in the kitchen. He noticed the gutted plastic cooking bags in the trash.

"I've got to talk to more of the eyewitnesses when they get home from work," he said.

"Uh-hm," she said.

"That means I'll be busy tonight."

"Ah," she said, pretending to have just gotten his drift.

She turned the dishwasher on fast load and walked with him into the bedroom. The air conditioner was already humming away in there; she must have switched it on earlier, while she was preparing supper. The wiliness of women. The malleability of afternoons.

The bed was unmade, and the closet door was hanging half open. Nudger kept a change of clothes at Claudia's, and he saw his two ties—one blue-striped, one brown—hanging on the hook inside the door. Only there were three ties on the hook; his two had been joined by a solid-red tie. He remembered the cigarette butt in the living room ashtray.

"Whose tie?" he asked casually. "A present for me?"

"Tie?" Claudia finished unbuttoning her dress and stepped out of it. "Oh, that belongs to Biff. He forgot it and I stuck it there."

"Biff?"

"Biff Archway. He teaches physical education out at Stowe School. He was here last night."

"And took off his tie? What else did he take off?" Nudger realized he was only half joking; there was an edge in his voice that surprised him.

Claudia paused in unhooking her bra, bent sharply forward at the waist, and stared at him with her elbows back and out, as if she were an elegant bird that had just touched down in the bedroom. "Nudger . . ." There was a dark warning in her eyes.

He got undressed silently, slowly, waiting for the bedroom to cool. The window unit seemed to be doing an exceptionally efficient job.

Well, maybe Claudia was right to caution him. He admitted to himself that he'd demonstrated unreasonable jealousy over practically nothing. Made a prime ass of himself, not for the first time. Okay, he'd messed up; the heat and the wine might have had something to do with it.

Still, that red tie, slung luridly over his own . . .

When he got into bed beside Claudia, she was nude on top of the covers. Her body was pale and slim, her hip bones prominent. She had teacup-sized, pointed breasts, and lean but shapely dancer's legs, though she had never danced. Nudger felt the increasing tightness in his throat, the warm stirring at the core of him. He stroked her shoulder, said, "Biff Archway?"

Claudia sighed loudly. More of a hiss, really. "Biff was in the neighborhood and dropped by to see me."

"And took off his tie."

"Nudger, you and I aren't married. We're not engaged. I don't wear your class ring, like the girls wear boys' rings at Stowe School, with adhesive tape wrapped around them so they fit. That's very possessive."

"Possessive? Sure. I thought we had an understanding. A commitment."

She smiled at him, then propped herself up on one elbow and leaned over and kissed him. He felt the soft pressure of her breast against his arm. Her long dark hair brushed the side of his neck, tickled. "We do have an understanding," she assured him.

"Did this Archway make advances?"

"Advances?" She fell back with her head on the pillow and stared straight up at the ceiling.

"You know. Advances . . ."

"Jesus, Nudger! Sometimes I think you live in the nineteenth century. No, he didn't make advances toward me; he came in here walking backward, and then he kind of sidled out."

"That's not a serious answer."

She turned her head and looked at him, a bit sadly, he thought.

"Seriously, I'm not going to answer you. You shouldn't have asked."

Nudger started to get out of bed. When he sat up he felt her hands on his shoulder, fingers clawing into his flesh, drawing him back. He sat for a long moment on the edge of the mattress, feeling her grip loosen.

Maybe he was making too much of all this. Maybe this Archway guy really did just happen to be in the neighborhood and dropped by, and it was hot so he removed his tie and it found its way into Claudia's bedroom. On top of Nudger's ties. Maybe. Nudger wondered if he should check the drawer where he kept his underwear.

He settled back down on the bed, amused at his own unreasonableness. Green-eyed fool Nudger.

Claudia wrapped her arms around him as he pulled the length of her lean body against him. The naked heat of her felt good in the cool room. They kissed, and he ran his fingertips ever so lightly over her erect nipples. She tossed her head and snuggled even closer against him.

Things were all right again.

Better than all right.

"So I'm a jealous middle-aged guy," Nudger said, after about ten minutes. "We get that way when we see the dark at the end of the tunnel."

She laughed softly, and he kissed her forehead and shifted so his body was poised above hers. The bed creaked, then was quiet, as if waiting.

"What else does this Archway teach out at the school?" Nudger asked.

"Physio-social analysis and adaptability."

"What's that?"

"Sex education."

Nudger rolled heavily to the side, said, *"Damn!"*

6

Edna Fine lived in the Hallmont Apartments, directly across the street from Olson's Liquor Emporium. Hers was a one-bedroom unit facing the street, and on the day of the murder she'd heard shots and looked out her window in time to see a man flee from the store, climb into a dark green car that was waiting for him at the curb, and fire a shot back from the speeding car as it left the scene. She'd told her story to the police, made her identification, given her deposition for the prosecution, and thought the affair was ended.

But here was Nudger, sitting across from her in her living room, asking questions. Pesky Nudger.

He smiled at Edna Fine and thought that she looked more like a middle-aged spinster than anyone he'd known. She was tall and unattractively angular, with a tiny pinched face, graying hair, and an austere look about her that suggested teetotaling, no sex except once during leap years, and stern morality in all matters. She wore rimless round glasses and had on a plain black dress suitable for funerals. A jury would sense that she might be bending over too far backward in her effort to smite evil, and might hear her testimony with some dubiousness if they saw her. The prosecutor knew what he was doing when he'd taken her deposition and merely had her sworn testimony read into the record, so she wouldn't actually appear in court. Colt's lawyer, a guy named Siberling, hadn't cross-examined her. Nudger would have to talk with Siberling.

Edna Fine's small, antiseptic apartment's furniture fit her appearance; it was dull, stiff, and unadorned. Nudger shifted uncom-

35

fortably on the wood-trimmed, straight-backed sofa and said, "Did you get a good look at the suspect's face, Miss Fine?"

"You mean Curtis Colt?"

Nudger nodded.

Edna Fine smiled.

Wait a minute. It changed her entire appearance, gave her surprising warmth. The pinched face widened, and crow's feet added humanity to the close-set blue eyes. Nudger liked her better. A jury might have, too; maybe the prosecutor had missed a good bet after all. And maybe Siberling had done some pre-trial investigation and was wise not to have put her on the stand.

She said, "Don't think I'm so cocksure of my identification that you have to humor me as if I'm some kind of tight-assed old maid."

Nudger was constantly amazed by how appearances could deceive. The world was made up of distorting mirrors, things were the opposite of what they seemed. "Then you're *not* sure?"

"I'm as sure as it says in my deposition. I went to the window after hearing shots, looked out, and saw this skinny little man carrying a gun run from the store and get into a car that drove away with him."

"How many shots did you hear?"

"Four, plus one when the car sped toward the corner. I knew they were shots immediately; I spent three years as a nurse in Southeast Asia and I recognize gunfire."

"And did you see the man's face?"

She sat down with an exaggerated, incongruous primness on a dainty chair facing the sofa and nodded. "Got a glimpse. What I saw mostly, though, was the top of his head. Mass of wavy dark brown or black hair. Parted in the middle, I think. He was a slender little bastard, but sort of wiry, strong-looking. Remember, though, I had to take all this in within about four seconds."

"But you picked Curtis Colt out of a police lineup."

She shrugged. "When I saw him standing there, it just hit me that he was the man. You want a drink, Mr. Nudger?"

"No, thanks." A scrawny yellow cat strutted into the room, angled over, and rubbed against Nudger's leg. Nudger was mildly surprised; the apartment smelled nothing like cat; it had in fact a faint lilac scent.

Edna Fine clucked her tongue at the cat and patted a hand on her bony thigh. The cat took two smooth leaps and was curled in her lap. "Matilda's hungry," she said.

Nudger wasn't surprised that the cat's name was Matilda. It was exactly the sort of name a lonely spinster would choose for a pet. At least that was consistent with his initial impression of Edna Fine, with the face and mannerisms she'd worn when she greeted him. "What did you see after the car drove away?" he asked.

"Just before it turned the corner, I saw Colt's arm come out the window and he fired a shot behind him." She twisted her body awkwardly to the left to mimic the action. Then she began absently stroking Matilda. "After that, I noticed a woman on the sidewalk just up the street from the liquor store. She was walking an ugly little brown dog on a leash. Langeneckert turned out to be her name—the woman's, not the dog's. Then two men came out of the store and looked up the street this way, in the direction the car had gone, and one of them ran back inside. That's when I turned away from the window and dialed nine-eleven for the police."

"Did anyone shout or say anything?"

"I think Mrs. Langeneckert yelled something as the car drove away, but I can't be sure. This apartment's almost soundproof. It's air-conditioned; the front windows don't even open."

Another cat, this one a big black-and-white tom with a pointy face, sauntered into the room, rubbed against Edna Fine's ankle, then stretched out at her feet.

"This is Artemas," she said. "He's part Abyssinian."

"Are there any others?" Nudger asked, wondering if Artemas was an Abyssinian name as well as Greek.

"Only Artemas and Matilda." She spoke of her pets as if they were her children—the old-maid characteristic of misplaced maternal affection. Or maybe she simply loved animals.

"Did you go downstairs after you called the police?" Nudger asked.

"No, I went back to the window and watched everything from there. A small crowd had gathered by that time. Within a few minutes the police and an ambulance arrived."

Nudger got up and walked across soft carpet to the living room window overlooking Gravois Avenue. It afforded an uncluttered view of the liquor store.

Olson's Liquor Emporium had a narrow front with two small display windows, but the building was long, with several high, grilled windows running along the side that Nudger could see. There were some red-lettered sale posters in the display windows, and a CLOSED sign was hanging crookedly in the window of the door. A man in a pale suit walked past the front of the store, got into a parked car, and drove away. Nudger had barely been able to make out his features.

The street was four lanes here, so the angle wasn't bad, but the distance was farther than Nudger had assumed. Edna Fine had the longest view of all the eyewitnesses, yet she seemed the one most likely to give an accurate account.

Nudger turned from his view of the dusk-shadowed street. "Is there any doubt in your mind that the man you saw was Colt?"

"Not much, Mr. Nudger."

"But some."

"There's a particle of doubt in my mind about almost everything. But I guess I'd give my deposition the same way today. Lawyers have a way of putting questions, don't they?"

"They do," Nudger agreed. "That's how innocent people get convicted sometimes."

"Sometimes, Mr. Nudger, but not this time. I don't believe in capital punishment; I've seen how any kind of killing usually begets more killing. But I still think Curtis Colt's guilty. And the law is . . ."

"The law," Nudger finished for her.

She nodded sternly, and magically the earthy reasonableness that made her likable disappeared. She became a self-righteous, worn woman who was sending a young man for a ride on the lightning. What a Jekyll and Hyde witness she would have made on the stand. "That's right, Mr. Nudger. And the law must have its due." She dumped Matilda onto the floor and stood up, tall, wise justice in a black dress. So unlike her other self. Her real self?

Matilda dejectedly left the room, then Artemas stretched, switched his tail, and followed.

Nudger knew it was time for him to leave, too.

He drove out to where Candy Ann Adams worked as a waitress at the Right Steer Steakhouse on Watson Road.

After pushing through plastic swinging doors manufactured to resemble Western saloon doors, he made his way through a modern glass door, then along a narrow railed area where customers were lined up and herded past the desserts, drinks, and cashier, and then were set out to graze at the salad bar in the middle of the Old West decor.

The manager, a young guy wearing a cheap straw ten-gallon hat and a cowboy shirt with "Trail Boss" embroidered over the pocket, told Nudger that Candy Ann had left just fifteen minutes ago because she wasn't feeling well. Nudger thanked him kindly, wishing he had a ten-gallon hat of his own to tip.

Leaving the warmth and slightly nauseating burned-steak smell of the Right Steer, he drove to Placid Grove Trailer Park.

The lights were burning in Candy Ann's trailer. Nudger pulled the Volkswagen up close to the metal wall near her door and turned off the sputtering engine. A lacy curtain parted in one of the windows.

She was standing holding the trailer door open when he unfolded up out of the car.

"C'mon in, Mr. Nudger. You learn anything?"

"Nothing you'll want to hear," he told her.

The light from the trailer's interior shone through her thin discount-store skirt, silhouetting her slender legs. Apparently she'd just finished washing her hair; there was a blue towel wound turban-style on her head. The top-heavy bulk of the wrapped towel made her body appear even thinner and somehow sensually awkward.

She stood aside as Nudger stepped up into the trailer and edged around her. She smelled like perfumed, soapy shampoo. It reminded him of how his former wife Eileen had smelled immediately after a shower. Still, he liked that scent.

Nudger sat in the vinyl chair again, and she settled into a corner of the undersized sofa, as she had the first night he'd been here; these things took on a certain convention. There was a jelly-jar glass half full of a clear liquid on the small table by the sofa. Nudger picked up another scent now. Alcohol. High-proof gin.

"I been drinking, Mr. Nudger," Candy Ann admitted. "Not much. Just enough to ease my headache some, and my worry about Curtis."

"I'm not going to be able to offer much comfort," Nudger told her. "I talked to the witnesses, and all of them stick to their stories." He told her the details of the conversations.

As she sat listening, she unwound the towel and began to rub her incredibly tangled wet blond hair, sending glistening clear water droplets flying. Her little-girl features were drawn into a pained and contemplative expression that made Nudger want to put his arm around her as a father might and pat her shoulder, assure her that everything would work out okay eventually, lie and lie and lie.

What he said was, "It only takes two witnesses to convict, Candy Ann. In this case there are four. And they're all solid. None of them is at all in doubt about his or her identification of Curtis Colt as the killer."

Candy Ann continued rubbing the rough towel on her scalp violently, as if she were determined to buff her hair from her head. Or her worries from her mind.

Nudger leaned forward, placed his elbows on his knees, and looked squarely at her. "I have to be honest; it's time you should face the fact that Colt is guilty and you're wasting your money on my services."

She stopped rubbing her wet hair, gazed at him with her pale blue eyes from beneath the folds of the damp towel. "All them witnesses know what's going to happen to Curtis," she said. "They'd never want to live with the notion they might have made a mistake, killed an innocent man, so they've got themselves convinced that they're positive it was Curtis they seen in that liquor store. They gotta be positive if they want to sleep at night."

"Your observation on human psychology is sound," Nudger said, "but I don't think it will help us. The witnesses were just as certain at the trial. I took the time to read the court transcript; the jury had no choice but to find Colt guilty, and the evidence hasn't changed. Nothing has changed, Candy Ann. . . ."

"That Randy Gantner, I think he'd just as soon see Curtis dead, knowing Curtis might do something even from prison to stop him from pestering me."

"Gantner pestered you?" Nudger sat back and felt warm vinyl attach itself to his perspiring back through his shirt. "How could he know where you live? How could he even know you exist?"

Candy Ann lowered her eyes. "I told him, I'm afraid. It was before I hired you; I thought maybe I could talk to them witnesses myself, get them to see Curtis' innocence, his goodness. Gantner's the only one I seen. After him, I knew how hopeless it was for me and that I needed the help of an expert." She looked up and smiled. "That's when I called you, Mr. Nudger."

"So Gantner found out where you lived."

"I ain't sure he knows where I live, but he came by the Right Steer a few times. He . . . made advances."

"That sounds like something out of the nineteenth century," Nudger said.

"Huh?"

"Never mind. What kind of advances?"

"Improper."

"Oh, I'm sure. But was the implication that if you slept with him he might change his story about Curtis?"

"No, he never came right out and said that." She rubbed her nose vertically with the palm of her hand, as a child might, and looked pensive. "Tell you the truth, Mr. Nudger, though I shouldn't say it—if it would really save Curtis' life, I'd even sleep with that Gantner. Would in a minute."

"I don't think it would make much difference," Nudger said. "And I don't think Curtis would approve."

"You're probably right about both those things."

Nudger shook his head slowly. "I'm sorry, but the evidence looks exactly the same as it did at the time of the trial."

Candy Ann drew her bare feet up off the floor and hugged her knees to her chest with both arms as if she were crazy about her legs. It was almost a gesture of unconscious, undeveloped sexuality, the sort of thing you might see in a ten-year-old. Her little-girl posture matched her little-girl faith in her lover's innocence. She believed the white knight must arrive at any moment and snatch handsome Curtis Colt from the electrical jaws of death. She believed hard, this child-woman. Nudger could almost hear his armor clank when he walked.

She wanted him to believe just as hard. "I see you need to be convinced of Curtis' innocence," she said wistfully. There was no doubt he'd forced her into some kind of a corner with his lack of faith and his disheartening report of unshakable witnesses. "If you come by here at midnight, Mr. Nudger, I'll convince you."

"Can't we make it earlier?" Nudger said. "My old car turns into a pumpkin at midnight."

She smiled slowly, her slightly protruding teeth separating her lips. "I seen cars was lemons, Mr. Nudger, but never pumpkins."

"How do you intend to prove Colt's innocence?"

"I can't say. You'll understand why later tonight."

"But why do we have to wait until midnight?"

"Oh, you'll see."

Nudger looked at the waiflike creature curled in the corner of the sofa. He felt as if they were playing a childhood guessing game while Curtis Colt waited his turn in the electric chair. Nudger had never seen an execution; he'd heard it took longer than most people thought for the condemned to die. There were spasms, wisps of smoke, the scent of charred flesh.

His stomach actually twitched. How did he ever get pulled into this case? How did he get pulled into this odd occupation? But he knew how. It had something to do with unpaid bills. And with other kinds of obligations. With not being able to walk away like a sane man. He'd be there at midnight.

"Can't we do this now with twenty questions?" he asked, trying one more time to get to bed early tonight.

Candy Ann shook her head. More drops of water flew, playing bright tricks with the lamplight. For a moment there was magic in the trailer. "No, Mr. Nudger. Sorry."

Nudger sighed and stood up, feeling as if he were about to bump his head on the low ceiling even though he was barely six feet tall. "All right, Candy Ann, we'll do it your way."

She smiled again, as if thanking him, as if he'd had a choice.

"Make sure you're on time tonight, Mr. Nudger," she called as he went out the door. "It's important."

Nudger wondered at the different worlds people lived in, while the real world had its way with them.

He didn't notice the car following him as he turned the Volkswagen out of the trailer park.

7

Nudger drove to his office to wait for midnight. He checked his phone-answering machine again. Another call from Eileen, who demanded in her no-nonsense voice that he call her back as soon as possible. He reached for the phone, almost lifted the receiver, then slowly drew his hand back and settled down in his swivel chair, which gave a soft little squeal, as if assuring him he'd been wise not to call. He didn't feel like talking to Eileen right now. Ever again, actually.

In the yellowish glow from his desk lamp, he leafed once more through his file on Curtis Colt, hoping he'd notice something he'd missed. But there was nothing pointing toward Colt's possible innocence. Probably because Colt was guilty.

After half an hour, Nudger closed the file folder and abruptly shoved it away from him on the desk. There was frustration and quiet despair in the gesture. He wished Danny's Donuts was open downstairs; he could use someone to talk to. The Cardinals were still playing phenomenal baseball and had won five games in a row now; Danny, who was an avid fan, would be happy to discuss baseball for the next few hours.

Or it might not hurt to talk with Danny about Curtis Colt. Danny was a good sounding board and sometimes provided insight. He tended to think in terms of stereotypes, but once he saw someone like Colt as an individual, his soft heart took over. Danny was all for capital punishment, but if Jack the Ripper had been someone he knew, Danny would have figured those girls did something to provoke him.

Curtis Colt was no mad-dog killer, nothing exceptional as criminals went; he was a garden-variety holdup man who had panicked and pulled the trigger when the job went sour. Or was he only that? There were disturbing reverberations around the shots he'd fired. Nudger decided he'd better learn more about Colt.

The phone jangled, startling Nudger. The swivel chair cried out as he sat up straight. Eileen? For a moment his hand hesitated, then he lifted the receiver and held it tight to his ear, as if there were someone in the quiet office he didn't want to overhear the conversation.

It wasn't Eileen on the line; it was Harold Benedict, of the law firm of Benedict and Schill, for whom Nudger sometimes did work. He said he'd been trying to contact Nudger all day.

"Why didn't you leave a message, Harold?" Nudger asked.

"You never answer your messages, Nudger. I don't know why you even have a recorder."

"I listen sometimes, I just don't call back. People who leave a message for you to call them back usually mean trouble. Besides, I don't like getting instructions from machines. But I'd have called you back because sometimes you pay me money."

"You're a throwback to the primeval days before microchips." Nudger had no reply for that. Pointless to deny. Lawyers.

Benedict told him a guy named Cal Smith had an insurance disability claim in for a back injury sustained on his job as a warehouse worker. The insurance company was a Benedict and Schill client, and Benedict didn't think Smith's back was really injured or that his client should pay the claim. A hard man was Benedict. And a devious one. He wanted Nudger to do some camera work.

Nudger had done this sort of thing before for Benedict and Schill. He wrote Smith's address on his desk pad, then hung up the phone.

Smith, he thought, sitting back in his chair. Maybe the most common name of all, the butt of low-comedy motel jokes. Nothing like the improbable Biff Archway. Nudger swallowed a bitter taste on the edges of his tongue. His stomach stirred like a cranky, disturbed beast. Was there really someone named Biff Archway?

But he knew there was, and that the person so named wore ties that found their way into Claudia's bedroom.

Nudger wondered what was the full given name of someone called Biff. He'd have to ask Claudia. And what would a Biff look like? Nudger had a good idea of that: a medium-height, chesty guy, with a firm jaw, clear eyes, and all-American charm. That was a Biff, all right. A regular guy John Wayne would have liked instantly.

Anger—no, not anger, jealousy—flared for a moment, but he pushed it away to a far corner of his mind where it could fester quietly while he went about his business. Claudia was right, he knew. She and Nudger weren't married or engaged, so maybe this was to be expected. She'd been a bird with a broken wing when he met her. He'd helped to heal the wing, and now she could fly. And maybe she wanted to soar for a while. Maybe it was as simple as that: the blood talking. Or the hormones.

Nudger peeled back the silver foil on a roll of antacid tablets and thumbed two of the chalky white disks onto his tongue. He chomped down on them hard, chewing loudly in the quiet, dimly lit office. The occasional whisper of traffic from the street below was the only reminder of an outside world.

It occurred to Nudger that perhaps Dr. Oliver, Claudia's analyst, who had helped her to get over the scars of her marriage to Ralph, had advised her to see other men. Part of her therapy. Oliver would do that, and the hell with Nudger if he thought it would help Claudia.

Or maybe this Biff Archway really was just a fellow teacher who'd been in the neighborhood and felt he should drop by to see a co-worker. Possibly he was a scrawny little wimp who loved only his mother. Little acne-pitted guy with an Oedipus complex. Could be. What the heck, give him crooked teeth and bad breath.

Nudger realized he was squeezing the edge of the desk so hard that his hands ached. His nails were dead-white out near the very tips of his fingers.

He loosened his grip and laughed out loud at himself. It was too loud and didn't sound like genuine laughter, but he told himself it should be genuine. He was acting like a paranoid adolescent jilted on the night of the prom.

The hell with this, he thought. He would phone Claudia and apologize to her for his fit of juvenile jealousy. They would talk for a while, come to an understanding, and he'd feel better.

He picked up the receiver again and tapped out her number.

Claudia's phone rang ten times. She wasn't home.

Nudger hung up. "Bullshit!" he said, loud enough to startle himself. He swallowed the jagged chunks of antacid tablet. They hurt his throat.

"You shouldn't oughta curse."

The squat, ugly little man who was standing a few feet inside the door wasn't joking. Simple sincerity oozed from him. He must have moved with supernatural quiet; Nudger looked closely to make sure his visitor cast a shadow. He seemed simply to have appeared there like a genie from a too-small lamp that had kept him cramped and mashed down for centuries.

He had a pushed-in, amiable face that was too large for his head but not large enough for his short, thick neck. The red Strohs Beer T-shirt he wore was stretched tight over bulging muscles and a bulging stomach paunch. If he'd been taller he'd have resembled one of those muscular, gone-to-fat pro wrestlers, but he was only about five feet four and merely looked pudgy and mildly dangerous; the Pillsbury Doughboy after weight training.

Nudger tilted the shade on the desk lamp so he could see the man more clearly. There was something vaguely familar in the dark hair and eyes, the confident, defiant set of the jaw. And something disturbingly vacant about the cast of the thickened features.

"I'm Lester Colt," the man said with a flat, southwest Missouri twang. "Curtis Colt's my little brother."

8

"How did you find out I was looking into your brother's case?" Nudger asked. "And how did you know I'd be in my office this late?"

Lester Colt walked farther into the office, grinning and hooking his thumbs in the wide belt of his threadbare Levi's. The belt featured a saucer-sized buckle engraved with a tractor-trailer. The buckle looked cheap but handcrafted, a beautiful bit of throwaway artistry. "Didn't know what kinda business you was in till I saw the lettering on your door. As to how'd I know you was here, I followed you from Candy Ann's place. Stuck to you like fresh-chewed gum." He seemed immensely proud of himself.

"I didn't hear you come up the stairs," Nudger said. The stairs, and the floorboards on the landing outside the door, squeaked loudly. Nudger liked them that way.

Lester shrugged, still grinning. "I snuck up."

"Why?"

"Wanted to see what kinda place I was in before I made myself known. I thought you was seeing Candy Ann on something other than business, Nudger. I see now I had you wrong, and her, too. She ain't as bad as I thought."

"You don't approve of Candy Ann?"

"I don't know. Don't matter much, anyways. At least it won't after next Saturday. I do think she oughta let Curtis be resting in his grave afore she carries on with somebody else. That Curtis, even though he was youngest, he did a good job of taking care of me when we was kids. Beyond then, even. I guess I owe it to him to see his girlfriend is treating him with the respect he deserves, despite the fact he's in the state prison.''

"I can assure you that she still loves Curtis," Nudger said. "What were you doing out at Placid Grove Trailer Park?" But looking at the shy, guarded expression on Lester's broad face, Nudger knew what. Lester might not entirely approve of Candy Ann Adams, but there was something about her that interested him.

"Passing by, is all," Lester said. "I thought I'd stop and talk to Candy Ann. Then I seen your car parked by her trailer, and I waited till you come out and wanted to find out who you was, so I drove behind you all the way into the city, then here." Again the pleased grin, the ignorance that was bliss. "Bet you didn't know I was behind you, even."

True enough; Nudger had hardly glanced in his rearview mirror, had simply driven along with his mind on other matters, blissfully ignorant in his own fashion.

He looked more closely at Lester, thinking of Ozark jug whiskey, kissin' kinfolk who didn't stop with kissing, and inbreeding that sometimes produced people like Lester Colt. Nudger figured Lester for the mentality of a cunning twelve-year-old.

"Do you drive a truck for a living?" Nudger asked, motioning toward the trucker's belt buckle.

Lester shook his head. "Naw, I ain't passed the chauffeur's-license test. But I will someday. I just load trucks now, is all." He put out a leg awkwardly, as if balancing himself against wind at a great height, and angled his chunky body toward Nudger, cocking his head and staring at an odd angle with wary, bewildered eyes. "You think you can help Curtis?"

Nudger silently cursed Candy Ann for raising false hope. "I doubt if I can help your brother, Lester. I'm simply going over the case again, on the off chance somebody overlooked something that might make a difference."

Lester nodded slowly. "I guess that oughta be done for Curtis. Candy Ann hire you?"

Nudger nodded.

Lester grinned again, his opinion of his would-have-been sister-in-law raised considerably. "You let me know if you hear anything new about Curtis," he said.

"Sure. Where can I get in touch with you?"

"I ain't got a phone, but I'm at Commerce Freightlines' warehouse down on Hall Street most days. On the loading dock."

Nudger made a show of writing that down on his notepad. "Okay, Lester."

Lester started to thank Nudger, but the words seemed too large for his larynx to handle. He nodded his slow, almost shy nod, and moved with surprising lightness toward the door. Then he turned. "You been to see Welborne?"

"Who?"

"Welborne's my other little brother. He's between me and Curtis. Might be you should talk to him." Lester sniffed and looked irritated. "That is, if he'll talk to you about Curtis."

"Doesn't he get along with Curtis?"

"Welborne don't get on with none of the family anymore; he don't see nobody. Curtis never went down home to see the folks hardly ever, either, but with him it was different. He's wild, I admit, but he's a good man, the best of all of us. Welborne, he just don't like going home, is all. Him and that snooty woman he married." Apparently Lester didn't like the idea of either of his brothers finding female companionship.

"Where can I locate Welborne?"

"He's a big-shot lawyer in Clayton someplace. I ain't even got his phone number; he won't give it to me." Anger shadowed Lester's beefy features. "Welborne coulda tried to help Curtis, but he didn't. That Siberling guy had to take the case."

"Were you at Curtis' trial?" Nudger asked.

"Sure I was. Every day. Even missed work. It was them witnesses did Curtis in."

"Do you think they were telling the truth?"

Lester frowned. "A person can think they're telling the truth and not be."

Lester was right about that, Nudger thought. It was what caused a lot of life's problems. "I'll find Welborne and talk to him," he said.

"If he'll talk to you," Lester repeated, and drifted out the door. Nudger didn't hear him light-foot it down the stairs, but the street door opened and clattered shut again. A draft stirred around Nudger's ankles.

There was no Welborne Colt in the phone directory. Sliding the Rolodex over to him, Nudger looked up Harold Benedict's home number and used a pencil to peck it out on the phone. Benedict's office was in Clayton, as were many law offices. If Welborne Colt practiced law from a Clayton office, Benedict might know him. Lawyers were thick as . . . well, thieves.

Benedict was home, and he had heard of Welborne Colt. He promised to get an address and phone number for Nudger by morning.

Nudger thanked him and replaced the receiver.

He felt his forehead; it was damp. The office seemed to be getting warmer, smaller. His stomach stirred and growled, reminding him that he'd had an early supper. He was more weak than hungry, but he knew he should get some food in the old machine. His night, pulsing with dark promise, might just be beginning.

He locked the office behind him, then left to treat himself to two White Castle hamburgers and a glass of milk before show-and-tell with Candy Ann Adams.

It was eleven-thirty by the time he topped the rise of the acceleration lane and drove fast with the windows open out the interstate toward Placid Grove Trailer Park. Static and soft blues were float-

ing from the radio and whirling on the wind and he could still taste
the hamburgers. Damned onions. Nudger belched. In the rearview
mirror the lighted city sank like a luminous dream, drawing down
with it the receding red taillights of cars that passed him going the
opposite direction. The taillights looked like streamers of bright
tracer bullets gracefully surrendering to gravity.

He glanced at his watch. He'd be early, but that was okay.
There was something about an appointment at midnight that
prompted punctuality.

9

At five minutes to midnight Nudger was sitting at the tiny table
in Candy Ann's kitchenette. Across from him sat a thin, nervous
man who might have been in his twenties, dressed in a long-
sleeved shirt despite the heat, and wearing sunglasses with silver
mirror lenses. Nudger didn't figure the glasses were to protect the
man's eyes from the sickly glare of the fluorescent light fixture set
in the trailer's ceiling.

Candy Ann introduced the man as "Tom, but that ain't his real
name," and said he was Curtis Colt's accomplice and the driver of
the getaway car on the night of the murder. He had to wait until
midnight to come so he'd be sure he wouldn't be seen.

It was all enough to make Nudger perk up his ears. He sat
quietly at the little table, looking into the mirrored glasses. He was
aware of a thousand crickets screaming like tortured souls outside,
Candy Ann's deep and regular breathing inside. Then she moved
back away from where she was standing close by his right shoulder, and he could hear his own breathing as he waited to listen to
what Tom had to say.

It was no surprise. "Me and Curtis was nowhere near the liquor store when them folks got shot!" Tom said vehemently, so forcefully that fine spittle flew across the table and coolly flecked Nudger's forearm.

Obviously the sunglasses were so Nudger couldn't effectively identify Tom if it came to a showdown in court. Tom had lank, dark brown hair that fell to below his shoulders, and when he moved his arm Nudger caught sight of something blue and red, like a faded nasty wound, on his briefly exposed wrist. But it wasn't a wound; it was a tattoo. Which explained the long-sleeved shirt worn in the sultry throes of summer.

"You can understand why Tom couldn't come forth and testify for Curtis in court," Candy Ann said.

Nudger said he could understand that. Tom would have had to incriminate himself. No fool, Tom.

"We was up on Parker Road, way on the other side of town," Tom said, "casing another service station, when that liquor-store killing went down. Heck, we never held up nothing but service stations. They was our specialty."

Which was true, Nudger had to admit. Colt had done a prison stretch for armed robbery after sticking up service stations. And all the other robberies he'd been tied to this time around were of service stations. The liquor store was definitely a departure in his MO, one not noted as such in court during Curtis Colt's rush to judgment.

"I'm looking at your hair," Nudger said.

"Huh? What about my hair?" Tom leaned his thin body back away from the table.

"It's in your favor. Your hair didn't grow that long in the time since the liquor-store killing. The witnesses described the getaway-car driver as having shorter, curlier hair, like Colt's, and a mustache."

"Tell you the truth," Tom said miserably, "me and Curtis was kinda the same type. So to confuse any witnesses, in case we got caught, I'd tuck up my long hair and wear a wig that looked like

Curtis' hair. Lots of people seen us like that. I burned the wig soon
as Curtis got arrested. My mustache was real, like Curtis'. I
shaved it off a month ago. We did look alike at a glance; sorta like
brothers. So my long hair ain't in my favor at all.''

Nudger bought that explanation; it wasn't uncommon for a team
of holdup men to play tricks to confuse witnesses and the police.
Too many lawyers had gotten into the game. The robbers, like the
cops, were taking the advice of their attorneys and thinking about a
potential trial even before the crime was committed. Nudger wondered if, in this pragmatic society, crime would someday become
respectable because of all the jobs it created.

Nudger looked at Tom. ''Is there any way you can prove you
were across town at the time of the murder?'' he asked, staring at
the two miniature Nudgers gazing back at him from the mirror
lenses.

''There's just my word,'' Tom said, rather haughtily.

Nudger didn't bother telling him what that was worth when it
came to checking the momentum of the wheels of justice; why
antagonize him?

''I just want you to believe Curtis is innocent,'' Tom said with
desperation. ''Because he is! And so am I!''

And Nudger understood why Tom was here, taking the risk. If
Colt was guilty of murder, Tom was guilty of being an accessory
to the crime. Once Curtis Colt had ridden the lightning, Tom
would have looming over him the possibility of an almost certain
life sentence, and perhaps even his own ride, if he was ever
caught. It wasn't necessary actually to squeeze the trigger to be
convicted of murder.

''I need for you to try extra hard to prove Curtis is innocent,''
Tom said. ''I'm asking you please not to give up on this case.''
His thin lips quivered, as if current were already singing through
them. He was near tears; he'd thought he was a big boy, but now
he was scared. He might be only in his early twenties behind those
disguising lenses, really just a frightened kid trapped by time and

circumstance. Nudger felt sorry for him; he should have felt sorrier for the old man and woman who'd been shot, but Tom was here, in front of him and looking into the black abyss. Every crime created its multitude of victims.

"Are you giving Candy Ann the money to pay me?" Nudger asked.

"Some of it, yeah." Tom sniffed and wiped his bony wrist across his nose, touched a finger up inside the mirror lenses as if scratching an itch. "From what Curtis and me stole. And I gave Curtis' share to Candy Ann, too. Me and her are fifty-fifty on this."

Dirty money, Nudger thought. Dirty job. Probably a hopeless job. Still, if Curtis Colt happened to be innocent, trying to prove it against the clock was a job that needed to be done. It would be a particularly tough job, considering the political climate; the powers-that-be wanted to send someone out via high voltage, and Curtis Colt was all but strapped in the chair for the final ride.

"Okay," Nudger said, "I'll stay on the case."

"Thanks," Tom said. His narrow hand crept impulsively across the table and squeezed Nudger's arm in gratitude, like the tentative hand of a lover. Tom had the sallow look of an addict; Nudger wondered if the long-sleeved shirt was to hide needle tracks as well as the tattoo.

Tom pushed away from the table and stood up, bravado in his exaggerated actions. The play he was starring in was good for at least another act; he was the desperado man of action again. These guys were all alike. He stood poised like a macho movie star about to spring into action on the "Late Show," a young Burt Lancaster but without the muscles and in ill health.

"Stay here with Candy Ann for ten minutes while I make myself scarce," he said. Not a bad line. Where was Denise Darcel? "I gotta know I wasn't followed. You understand it ain't that I don't trust you; a man in my position has gotta be sure, is all."

"I understand. Go."

Tom gave a spooked smile, like a wary animal sprung from a trap, and slipped out the door. Nudger heard his running footfalls on the gravel outside the trailer. Nudger was forty-three years old and ten pounds overweight; lean and speedy Tom needed a ten-minute head start like Sinatra needed singing lessons.

After a few minutes, the crickets began screaming again outside, a shrill expression of everybody's desperation. Tom had gotten clear, but he would never really be free.

"Is Tom a user?" Nudger asked Candy Ann.

"Sometimes. But my Curtis never touched no dope."

"You know I have to tell the police about this conversation, don't you?"

Candy Ann nodded. "That's why we arranged it this way. They won't be any closer to Tom than before."

"They might want to talk to you, Candy Ann."

She shrugged her thin shoulders. "It don't matter. I don't know where Tom is, nor even his real name nor how to get in touch with him. And he's got no reason to get in touch with me. He'll find out all he needs to know about Curtis by reading the papers."

"Do you know that Lester Colt followed me when I left here earlier this evening?"

"Lester? Curtis' brother?"

"That's the Lester."

"He's harmless, but he ain't quite right in the head. Ain't been since he was born, I been told. He's Curtis' big brother, but he's always been more like a little brother. What was he doing around here?"

"My impression is he's smitten with you and wanted to see you."

"Me? Lester has a crush on me?" Her eyes opened so wide, the whites were visible all around the blue irises. She seemed astounded.

"And he has fierce loyalty for Curtis. He thinks you shouldn't see any other men while Curtis is alive, or until a respectable time has passed if they do execute Curtis.''

"Curtis took good care of Lester when they was kids," Candy Ann said. "Looked out for him. Lester ain't bright, but he's smart enough to remember that. Down deep, Curtis is a decent man, Mr. Nudger. The most decent I ever met.''

Nudger stood up. "I thought you should know about Lester's feelings, and about the fact that the police might want some of your time.''

"I can handle both those problems, Mr. Nudger." There was coy confidence in her little-girl smile. Undoubtedly she'd been the one who'd worked out the details of his conversation with Tom in such a way that Tom remained safe from the law. And her method was effective; there was no way to wring Tom's whereabouts out of her, or even prove the midnight conversation had taken place.

"You have a surprisingly devious mind," Nudger told her, "considering that you look like Barbie Doll's country kid cousin.''

Candy Ann smiled wider, surprised and pleased. Looking at her made Nudger think of misty pastures and buttermilk biscuits and fields of bright sunflowers. And even with that she managed to stir a raw carnal yearning. She was one of those rare women with a direct line to the male libido. Possibly it made little difference what she looked like; something in her sent out arousing vibrations.

"Do you think I'm attractive, Mr. Nudger?" She asked it as if she really didn't know the answer.

"Yeah. And painfully young."

For just a moment Nudger almost thought of Curtis Colt as a lucky man. Then he looked at his watch, saw that his ten minutes were about up, and said good-bye. He felt old, old. . . .

If the Barbie Doll had a kid cousin, the Ken Doll probably had one somewhere, too. And time was something you couldn't deny. Ask Curtis Colt.

10

Nudger was up early the next morning, sitting in the Volkswagen on Page Boulevard with his camera, a cup of lukewarm coffee, and breakfast. The camera was a 35-millimeter Minolta equipped with an 80–200-millimeter zoom lens. Breakfast was an Egg McMuffin.

From where he was parked, he could see the run-down neighborhood in the next block, the back and side of Calvin Smith's small, white-frame subdivision house. Smith was the warehouseman Benedict was sure was perpetrating an insurance fraud. There were some lawn chairs on a makeshift brick patio, a black kettle barbecue pit, and a rusty '68 Buick up on blocks in the backyard. In the carport sat Smith's ten-year-old Chevy. The guy looked almost as broke as Nudger; for a moment Nudger considered driving away and letting him collect his insurance settlement for his injured back. Even if he didn't have an injured back.

Nudger finished his Egg McMuffin, brushed butter and crumbs from his fingers, and sipped his coffee. Rush-hour motorists stared at him curiously as they drove past on their way to work. It was a matter of time before a cop would happen along, stop, and demand to know what Nudger was doing parked here. Long, dubiously accepted explanations would ensue, maybe a phone call to Benedict and Schill. It might take most of the morning to sort things out.

Even where Nudger sat, with all the traffic noise, he heard the door in the next block slam, like a gunshot signaling the start of an event. The Smith family was up and moving; the game had begun.

He put down his coffee, spilling most of it on the rubber floor mat, and picked up the camera.

Just as Harold Benedict had predicted, Calvin Smith's wife was leaving for her job with a vending-machine company. Calvin, a big, tousle-haired man wearing work pants and a white T-shirt with somebody's photograph—it looked like Bruce Springsteen's—emblazoned on the chest, lumbered after her out onto the carport and bent to kiss her good-bye.

The side door slammed again, and a five- or six-year-old boy came bounding out of the house like a joyous puppy sensing space to romp. The wife, a heavyset woman in white slacks she should have known better than to wear, got into the car and started the engine.

Calvin seemed to move okay for a guy with a bad back; he walked around the car and leaned on the window frame, talking to his wife. Nudger got a shot of that, twisted the lens, and zoomed in tighter.

Calvin stepped away and the wife swiveled her head and began backing the car out of the driveway.

Just then the kid started to gallop around the rear of the moving car to return to the house. Calvin Smith took several catlike strides, stooped low, and scooped the boy up out of real or imagined harm. The camera clicked and the winder whirred three times, freezing the surprising suppleness and grace of the big man, recording the death of an insurance claim; poverty in motion.

After a sudden stop and some head-shaking, Mrs. Smith backed the rest of the way into the street and drove away. Calvin, carrying the boy easily under one arm, walked to the patio and tossed a clear plastic cover over the barbecue pit, slid some aluminum lawn chairs back against the house, then went inside. The camera followed him all the way, dooming his insurance claim for sure, maybe laying some legal problems on him if Benedict and Schill wanted to get nasty. And they could get nasty.

Nudger would have the photographs developed by afternoon and get the prints to Harold Benedict. A job well done; easy money for a change. But Nudger drove away not feeling good about it.

After dropping the film off at the lab, he cut over Shrewsbury to Highway 44 and headed east, toward downtown and the Third District station house. Time to share.

"It doesn't wash with me," Hammersmith said from behind his desk, puffing angrily on his cigar. Angrily because it did wash a little bit; he didn't like the possibility, however remote, of sending an innocent man to his death. That was every good homicide cop's nightmare, the thing that would render the hunter not so unlike the hunted. "This Tom character is just trying to keep himself clear of a murder charge."

"You could read it that way," Nudger admitted.

"You could be an illiterate and you'd have to read it that way," Hammersmith said. "In any language."

Nudger thought the language would make no difference to an illiterate, but he kept quiet.

"It would help if you gave us a better description of Tom," Hammersmith said gruffly, as if Nudger were to blame for Curtis Colt's accomplice still walking around free.

"I gave you what I could," Nudger said. "Tom didn't give me much to pass on. He's streetwise and scared and knows what's at stake."

Hammersmith nodded, his fit of pique past. But the glint of weary frustration remained in his eyes. He inhaled deeply on the cigar, blew a noxious cloud of greenish smoke. Pollution personified.

"You going to question Candy Ann?" Nudger asked.

"Sure, but it won't do any good. She's probably telling you straight. Tom would figure we'd talk to her; he wouldn't let her know how to find him. And she wouldn't want to know where he was. If she's Curtis Colt's girl, she knows the rules and would probably drive a polygraph operator to distraction with nothing but the useless truth."

"You could stake out her trailer."

"Do you think Candy Ann and this Tom might be lovers?"

"No."

Hammersmith gazed down at his smoldering cigar and shook his head. "Then they'll probably never see each other again. And if they do, it might not be for months, even years. Watching her trailer would be a complete waste of manpower, and that's a commodity the taxpayers have left me short of."

Nudger knew Hammersmith was right. The St. Louis Police Department, like the police of most major cities, had an oversupply of crime and an undersupply of men. "What can you tell me about Colt's lawyer?" he asked.

"Charles Siberling. A young guy from Legal Aid. But don't get any ideas about Colt getting the shaft because of inadequate counsel. This Siberling is young, but he's smart and part shark, making a reputation in this town. Quite the cocky little bastard; he's even been known to show up his partners, who aren't regarded as fools."

"He's with a law firm?"

"Uh-huh. Elbert and Stein, over in the Pennwright Building in lawyer-glutted Clayton. His Legal Aid work is done on the side; Elbert wants him to get courtroom experience before he does something really important like defend some big shot's tax write-off."

"You seem to know a lot about Siberling," Nudger said.

Hammersmith deliberately blew smoke in Nudger's direction; Nudger thought he saw a mosquito go down. "He's the kind of lawyer who's going to be a pain in the ass for a long time. Shaw is the top criminal lawyer in this town now; Siberling figures to be the next in line. I feel confident in making that prediction, despite his youth and inexperience. He's got star quality and an instinct for sniffing out weakness."

"He wasn't much help to Curtis Colt."

"Which oughta tell you something, Nudge."

The smoke was getting to be too much to bear. Nudger knew his sport coat would reek of it until the dry cleaner down the street from his office gave out coupons again. He stood up to go.

"What are you going to do now?" Hammersmith asked.

"I'll talk to the witnesses again. I'll go see Siberling. I'll read the court transcript again. And I'd like to talk with Curtis Colt."

"They usually don't allow visitors on Death Row, Nudge, only temporary boarders."

"This case is an exception," Nudger said. "Will you try to arrange it?"

"Siberling would be the guy to do that; he's still Colt's lawyer."

"You were in charge of the investigation, and you have connections a young lawyer hasn't heard about. I'll ask Siberling, but I'd like to be able to tell him you're working on it, too."

Hammersmith chewed thoughtfully on his cigar, making the end of the thing a soggy greenish mess. Since he'd been the officer in charge of the investigation, he was the one who'd nailed Curtis Colt. That carried an obligation, a responsiblity. For a cop like Hammersmith, that responsibility could turn into a cross that would weigh him down for the rest of his career, that he might eventually bend under.

Years ago, Hammersmith and Nudger had known a police lieutenant named Billy Abraham who had sent an innocent woman to prison. The woman had hanged herself a week before someone else confessed to her crime. She had left a sealed note to Abraham that only he had read. Two days later Abraham had eaten his gun—cop talk for placing the barrel of his Police Special in his mouth and blowing off the top of his head. A messy as well as sudden way to find peace.

Nudger and Hammersmith looked at each other, thinking of Abraham.

"Tell Siberling nothing about me," Hammersmith said. "But I'll see what I can do. For you, Nudge, not for that little prick Siberling."

"For Curtis Colt."

"No," Hammersmith said. "Colt's guilty. And he's already got one foot in the next world; high voltage is going to goose him the rest of the way out of this one."

Nudger didn't argue with Hammersmith; the lieutenant was probably right. Needed to be right about Colt's guilt.

"I'll phone you soon," Hammersmith said, "let you know."

Nudger thanked Hammersmith, left the office, and walked down the hall into the clear, breathable air of the booking area. Ellis the desk sergeant let him use the wall phone usually reserved for suspects.

Nudger stood wearily before the grimy wall's display of desperately scrawled phone numbers of lawyers, relatives, and bondsmen, the graffiti of fear.

He used the dog-eared directory, dialed, and made an appointment to see Charles Siberling.

11

Mr. Siberling had an important court date that morning, a secretary at Elbert and Stein told Nudger. She had penciled Nudger in for an afternoon appointment but said she could make no promises; Mr. Siberling was running tight, schedule-wise. She actually said that, "schedule-wise." Nudger told her there was a great deal of money at stake, not to mention the political destinies of famous people. She said she couldn't guarantee him an appointment promise-wise, but it was almost a certainty that Siberling or one of the other partners would see him. Nudger told her only Siberling would do, and she sighed and said okay, crisply commanded him to have a nice day, and hung up the phone. He was left with the impression that she might be making sport of him.

After leaving the Third District station, Nudger drove west on Chouteau and stayed on it after it became Manchester and speared through the faltering heart of the near-suburb of Maplewood. He left the Volkswagen parked across the street by a broken meter, timed the flow of traffic, and jogged across sun-heated pavement toward his office, ignoring a few blaring horns and some imaginative cursing.

Even that slight exertion left him breathing rapidly, reminding him he was middle-aged and ought to be in some business requiring little effort other than sitting up now and then to count money.

He was about to enter the door to the stairs leading to his walk-up office when Danny rapped on the doughnut-shop window, just a few feet away. When he was sure he had Nudger's attention, Danny leaned forward over the window counter so he could see more clearly through the grease-spotted glass, then, with an urgent expression on his basset-hound features, he motioned for Nudger to come inside.

Nudger stood with the doughnut-shop door half open. As usual, there were no customers in the place. Pastry was mum; Danny could talk freely.

"A guy's upstairs waiting for you," he said in a modulated voice, leaning back so he was half sitting on one of the red vinyl counter stools. His eyes darted momentarily upward; if the walls didn't have ears, the ceiling might. Danny nervously wiped his fingers on his grayish towel. "Heavyset guy wearing jeans and a sleeveless T-shirt. Looks like the trouble type."

"How long has he been up there?" Nudger asked.

"That's just it; I saw him go in and heard him take the stairs about an hour ago, and he hasn't come down."

Nudger was trying to remember if he'd locked his office door last night. His memory couldn't reconstruct his exit accurately enough for him to be sure if he'd keyed the dead bolt.

"The guy looked like he was used to heavy work, or maybe lifted weights," Danny said.

"Did he have a stomach paunch?"

"Yeah, I guess so."

Nudger relaxed. T-shirt and jeans, muscular and paunchy. Lester Colt, probably sitting on the landing outside the office door and waiting for Nudger with simple, tireless patience. "It's okay, Danny," Nudger said, "I know who he is."

"In that case," Danny said, "shut the door; you're lettin' the air-conditioning out."

The narrow stairwell was dim after the brightness of late morning. The bare, low-wattage fixture that burned twenty-four hours a day on the high ceiling above the landing glowed like a distant star that shed only inconsequential light in this galaxy. The landing itself was in deep shadow. Nudger waited a few seconds for his eyes to adjust before he began climbing the stairs. A stale, perfumed scent wafted down to him, like the wake of cheap deodorant.

Lester wasn't waiting on the shadowed landing; apparently Nudger had neglected to lock the office door. He often forgot about locking the door. He'd obtained some interesting clients that way.

As he opened the door he noticed the looseness of the knob. But he was a step inside before it registered: the lock had been forced. He turned and saw that the doorjamb was splintered at eye level where the dead-bolt lock had been whittled loose higher on the door than the latch lock.

The door came alive in his hand and jumped closed.

The man who'd been standing behind it was heavyset and muscular, but not what you'd call paunchy; he looked as if he lived on yogurt and raw meat. He was at least six foot three, with a full-back's muscles straining the fabric of his red T-shirt. He had arms the size of legs. He was lean-waisted and broad-shouldered and lantern-jawed and not Lester Colt. A different sort of animal entirely.

Worst of all was the way he was smiling. It was the kind of smile you saw sometimes after hearing the dirtiest of dirty jokes. Like a crack in the curtains of a room where something basic and lewd was happening.

Nudger started to back up a step, but a huge hand darted out in an oddly lazy fashion and caught him on the side of the neck, driving him farther into the office. He skidded, caught his balance, and something like a bowling ball with knuckles rammed him in the chest. Air exploded from him and he was aware of saliva dribbling down his chin. He felt two more hard blows to the lower ribs, and he sank slowly to his knees, like a horse he'd once seen shot in the head. He seemed a distant party to what was going on; there was no pain, only numbness. He tried to get up, but his legs wouldn't respond and he wound up merely windmilling his arms and looking silly, like something built for the ground but trying to fly.

Vaguely he felt two more punches, this time to the head. The last one only grazed his ear and did bring a slice of hot pain. Each time the big man threw a punch he grunted loudly; it was more a grunt of animal pleasure than of effort. The ear continued to burn and Nudger somehow got his arms up over his head and started to roll into a protective ball.

But the grunter had feet and knew how to use them. He was an Astaire of destruction. Nudger experienced the same merciful numbness, but he was sure he heard a rib crack as the toe of a hard leather boot found him where he was most vulnerable.

Then he was yanked to his feet. The camera he'd used that morning was still strapped around his neck. His assailant grabbed it and laughed loudly, having a high old time. He twisted the strap about Nudger's neck, then began swinging him around like a bucket on a rope. Nudger heard himself gasp for breath as he stumbled in a circle, scrambling wildly to keep his balance. The revolving office began to fade into a deep and dizzying blackness pinpointed with beautiful, silent explosions of red, like hundreds of roses that kept blooming and blooming.

The strap, or one of the brackets where it was attached to the camera, broke. Nudger flew like something discarded into a corner, slumped on the floor, and began a rasping struggle for oxygen. Through hazed and distorting eyes he saw the big man hurl the camera onto the desk, pick it up and slam it down again, grunting as it broke into pieces that slid onto the floor. The guy sure liked to break things.

He walked over to Nudger, bent low, and gripped the front of Nudger's shirt, wadding it into a ball that tightened the fabric and made Nudger's head loll back. "Can you hear me?" he asked in a surprisingly soft voice. The words seemed muffled by distance.

Nudger somehow managed a ludicrous nod.

"A message from Western Union," the man said, grinning. He was witty as well as muscular. His breath smelled as bad as his deodorant, only different. "Back off the case, asshole. You understand? Leave it alone. Com-fuckin'-pletely alone."

He stood up, seeming to float, and Nudger, with that odd numbness, felt the back of his head hit the floor and bounce.

"You understand?" a voice asked from up near the ceiling.

"Complete fuckly alone," Nudger stammered, wondering if the hoarse, dutiful voice was his own.

"No. *com*-fuckin'-*pletely* alone." Trying to be patient.

"Fuck . . . com . . . 'lone."

"Oh, well. You got the message."

A boot toe dug into Nudger's thigh; there was another low, primal grunt.

After a moment Nudger heard the rear window scrape-squeak open. The big guy had figured it all out; he was parked in back and had known from the beginning he was going to use the fire escape to leave.

Nudger listened to the faint ringing clatter of leather heels on the steel fire escape, the muted metallic scream of the drop ladder levering down to the alley. Then he heard nothing but a high-pitched buzzing that he knew was inside his head, and he sank into a cold and dark place that scared him.

"I thought somebody was playing racquetball upstairs," Danny was saying next to Nudger. Nudger sat with his eyes closed, concentrating on not letting the pain make him vomit. He was in a soft seat that vibrated and rocked; there was a low humming sound. A car engine. He slowly opened his eyes.

He was slumped low in the passenger seat of Danny's old blue Plymouth. So low that he couldn't see much out the windshield except the tops of trees and telephone poles zipping past.

Danny glanced over, caught his eye, and smiled his sad hound smile. But there was concern in his watery brown eyes. And something else. Anger.

"The guy had already got out the back way, Nudge," Danny said. "I didn't call the police; I figured I oughta ask you about that first. I couldn't identify him anyway, didn't even get a look at his car. And I only got a glimpse of him earlier when I seen him go up to your office. He musta been driving away while I was running up the front steps to see what all the bumping and bouncing around upstairs was."

"It was me," Nudger said. He raised his head to look around. A pain like a sharp slab of ice cut deep into his right side and made him suck in his breath.

Danny's pale right hand patted him gently on the knee. "You okay, Nudge?"

"My guess is that I'm not." His head began pounding with slow-pulsing force, as if someone were hammering long nails into his temples. "Where are we?" *Pound! Pound! Pound!*

"On the Inner Belt. I'm taking you to the County Hospital emergency room. You need some X rays. And they'll give you some pain pills." Dr. Danny. "Guy did a job on your camera, Nudge. I cleaned up the pieces."

Nudger didn't answer. He settled deeper into the Plymouth's worn upholstery and closed his eyes again, trying to stay as detached as possible from his throbbing head, from the playfully malicious pain that moved around his body and seemed to take a bite here, a bite there.

The message the human mountain had delivered to him was clear only up to a point. Had the man set out to smash Nudger's camera in order to expose the film? Or had he simply found himself holding the camera after the strap broke and in his orgy of destruction hurled it down on the desk? He might not know that Nudger had already dropped off the Smith shots at a film lab, that Nudger always reloaded his camera immediately after removing film, that the film in the camera was a fresh, unused roll.

Nudger had to consider the man's emphatic warning. "Hero" was a title he didn't particularly want. It was so often preceded by "dead." But even if he wanted to back away from the case rather than face another beating, he couldn't do it.

His problem was that he didn't know which case the big man had warned him about.

If it was the Smith case, the man's visit had been too late. The photos of Calvin Smith scooping up his kid and carrying him around were probably developed and printed by now, and would soon be in the clever hands of Harry Benedict.

Once Smith realized that, it would be pointless to have Nudger beaten again unless for the pure pleasure of revenge. And a pro like the bone crusher who'd plied his trade on Nudger didn't work cheap.

Nudger hoped the case in question was the Smith matter; not only would he see no more of his violent caller, but Benedict and Schill would pay the portion of Nudger's medical expenses not covered by insurance.

But if it was the Curtis Colt case he'd been warned to get out of, Nudger was probably still in danger. Because he wouldn't back away from that one.

He swallowed, fighting down the nausea that was hitting him now in waves. Persistence was all he seemed to have left in this confusing world; it was his constant, his religion. It was what his half-assed occupation was about, and somehow it had become what *he* was about. The sick and wrong ones could crush and grind him until he had nothing left but the ability to breathe. He would be scared and his stomach would turn on itself like coiled cable and he'd walk in where even fools feared to tread. Because he knew this about himself: if he couldn't make himself crawl back to the dotted line, he was nothing. Everything else had been taken away from him. His work was the albatross around his neck that sustained him.

He was on the Curtis Colt case at least until Saturday, when there would be no more Curtis Colt.

The car slowed, then rocked to a stop. Nudger opened his eyes and saw a sun-brightened brick wall with half a dozen fingers of grasping ivy growing up it, a bank of wide, green-tinted glass doors with gently sloping ramps leading to them. A brilliant monarch butterfly touched down for a second on the ivy, thought better of it, and fluttered away.

"We're here, Nudge," Danny said. "I'll come around and help you out."

But Nudger had already opened the passenger-side door and was sitting straddling a yellow line in the parking lot.

12

A Filipino doctor and a husky blond nurse argued about Nudger's X rays. Nudger and another emergency patient, a calm man with a fishhook in his arm, watched as the nurse kept trying to poke at the X rays with her finger while the doctor waved them around. Finally they decided that one of Nudger's lower ribs might be cracked. They also thought he might have suffered a concussion.

The guy who'd beat him up had been very professional. He could have hurt Nudger much more seriously. Nudger's face was unmarked except for a long red scratch, probably from a thumbnail, leading to his mangled and swollen right ear. There were fast-developing, huge bruises on his sides and on his right leg, where he'd been kicked. He was colorful.

County Hospital decided to keep him overnight for observation. They asked him if there was anyone he wanted notified of his whereabouts, but he said no. Claudia didn't have to know about this. A cheerful nurse woke him three times during the night, probably to assure him that he really was being observed.

When they released him in the morning, Danny was there to help him ease his stiffened body into the old Plymouth. Then they drove to Nudger's apartment on Sutton.

"Want me to help you get situated, Nudge?" Danny asked, after assisting him up the stairs and opening the door. It had been a long climb; they were both breathing hard and perspiring.

"I can make it okay, Danny. Thanks for all your trouble."

Concerned and embarrassed, Danny mumbled something about what friends were for and started to back away.

"How about coming in for some coffee?" Nudger asked, leaning on the door to take weight off his aching leg. "You can have some breakfast if you want, but I'm not up to it."

"Thanks," Danny said, "but I gotta go. Dunker Delite sale. I put a coupon in the local newspaper. Buy one, get one free."

Nudger nodded and watched him go back downstairs to the vestibule, then push out into the morning heat to walk to his car parked illegally in front of the building. He wondered if Danny knew that most customers wouldn't dream of eating a second Dunker Delite. Probably he didn't, and Nudger would be the last to tell him.

It was hot in the apartment, too. And the air was still and stale.

Nudger limped to the thermostat and adjusted it so the air-conditioning clicked on, then he made his way into the kitchen and got Mr. Coffee going. Things were bustling, all right. The pain in his side started to catch up with him as he lurched into the bathroom.

He got undressed slowly, with a great deal of agony, then stood in front of the mirror and gingerly untaped his ribs. Moving like a man made of glass, he bent over the tub and turned on the shower. When the water was plenty hot, he supported himself with a hand on the porcelain towel rack, maneuvered his way into the tub, and stood in the blast of hot water and rising steam.

After adjusting the angle of his body so the needle stings of water didn't beat on his injured rib, he began to relax.

He stayed in the shower for almost half an hour, until the water began to turn cool. Then he stepped out of the tub, switched on the exhaust fan to clear the bathroom of steam, and carefully rewrapped his torso. He wanted to lie down for the remainder of the day, and knew that he probably should, but he couldn't rest until after Saturday. Then he and Curtis Colt could rest uninterrupted for a long time.

Nudger stayed in his white terry-cloth bathrobe and sat barefoot in the kitchen while he ate toast with strawberry jam on it and drank three cups of strong black coffee. He listened to some FM jazz for a while on the radio, then tuned to KMOX and caught the hourly news. The Cardinals had won yet another ball game. Other than that, things were grim all over the map. It cheered Nudger perversely to realize that there were millions of people in the world worse off than he was.

He felt better and was moving more easily, if still slowly, as he went into the living room to use the phone.

Siberling's secretary was mad. Nudger had missed his appointment, actually stood up the prestigious firm of Elbert and Stein. It must have been like a slap in the face. No, Mr. Siberling wouldn't be in anymore today. Nudger tried honesty and explained to her that he wanted to talk to Siberling about Curtis Colt, and time was fleeting. She was unimpressed but said she would leave a message for Mr. Siberling. Nudger got the impression that, like Curtis Colt, he'd have to murder someone to get to see Siberling. He had a victim in mind.

After hanging up the phone, he sat for a few minutes, then lifted the receiver again.

If one lawyer wouldn't do, he'd try another.

Welborne Colt was easier to see than Charles Siberling. There was no one else in his office in the Belmont Building on South Central in Clayton. His partners, the "Edmundsen and Keane" lettered above "Colt" on the frosted glass door, were at lunch, Colt explained. As were the secretary and paralegal who usually sat at the semicircular desk in the reception area. The building was full of lawyers' offices; at first Colt thought Nudger had wandered in by mistake, someone else's client. When Nudger mentioned Curtis' name, Colt's gaunt, strong features darkened and his body tensed, but he smiled.

"Who hired you to hash over my brother's case?" he asked.

"A woman who cares about him," Nudger said. You had to play your cards tight with these legal types.

"I see. What happened to your ear, Mr. Nudger?"

"An accident. I was listening to Tina Turner and the earphone on my Walkman exploded."

Colt grunted and nodded. He knew when not to press. He walked across the plush carpet of the reception area to the window, then studied something down in the street. He was a tall man, but built wiry like his brother Curtis. There was a muscular bounce to his walk. He had hair like Curtis', too, dark and wavy, only his was styled shorter, razor-groomed, and receding and swept back in a way that lent him a dashing matinee-idol look that was almost caricature.

"I wondered why you weren't in on your brother's defense," Nudger said, not very tactfully but to the point.

Colt turned and gave him a measured look that he had probably practiced before the mirror as a law student. Great eyebrow work. "We do corporation work here, Mr. Nudger, not criminal law." There was the barest trace of Ozark twang in his voice.

"Some might say that's a contradiction in terms."

"Sometimes it is," Colt said.

"Have you been in touch with Charles Siberling?"

"Curtis' attorney? No, I haven't." He appeared uncomfortable, then leaned his weight far back on his heels and tucked the fingertips of both hands into the vest pockets of his three-piece, pinstripe lawyer's uniform. It was a portly old man's posture that didn't look right on a lean young man. "Curtis . . ." he said thoughtfully. "Crazy bastard wouldn't settle down. Couldn't."

"Why not?"

Welborne Colt straightened up and removed his fingertips from his pockets, as if his stance were a pose he could affect only so long. He shrugged. It was one of the most elegant shrugs Nudger had ever seen; Welborne was young and limber inside his skin again. "Who knows? We didn't come from a wealthy family, Mr. Nudger. My father sacrificed to send me to college at the state university, and he never let me forget it. Him and my momma, neither."

The abrupt country dialect startled Nudger. It went like a black roach on a white rug.

"You were the oldest brother," Nudger said. He didn't mention Lester. "So Curtis never had the same opportunity. That's the way it is in some families."

Welborne smiled and shook his head. "The little shit had opportunity. Made straight As in high school when he wasn't jerking around with junk cars and becoming part of the drug scene. There's a college near Branson, Missouri, Mr. Nudger, The School of the Ozarks. It's self-sufficient; the students farm it and take care of the livestock while they study agriculture. It's a damned good school. Curtis had himself a scholarship to go there, but he didn't even bother taking them up on it. Didn't even bother showing up to graduate from high school."

"Maybe he didn't want to ranch or raise corn."

"Wanted to raise hell is what Curtis wanted. What he did. Especially after coming to the city."

"Have you seen him since the trial?"

"No. I don't want to see him, and I don't think he'd want to see me. There's bad blood between us."

"He's your brother," Nudger said. "They're going to execute him. That's a forever thing."

"He did it to himself, Mr. Nudger. The way once a cue ball is stroked by the stick in a certain direction, everything is inevitable. It's going to bounce off a cushion, strike this ball at an angle and send it into that ball, and send that ball into another ball that will drop into a pocket. Curtis set his own direction and destiny early; what happened to him was in his future the way the pocket is in the future of a billiard ball."

Nudger stood mystified, glad Welborne Colt wasn't defending him in court. "Life isn't a pool table, Welborne."

Colt smiled handsomely, sadly. "Isn't it?"

"Do you believe Curtis is guilty of murder?"

"If a jury found him guilty, he killed that old woman."

"Juries have been wrong a few times."

"They're not wrong in Curtis' case. And if they'd found him not guilty, it would only have postponed the inevitable."

Billiard balls again. "Do you know Candy Ann Adams?"

"No. And I wouldn't know her if she's a friend of Curtis. We didn't have much to do with each other after I got out of southwest Missouri."

"Are you ashamed of your hillbilly origins, Mr. Colt?"

Welborne glared at Nudger. "You're a direct bastard, aren't you?" He rotated his wrist and glanced at the gold Rolex watch peeking out from beneath his white French cuff. "Let's see you be even more direct. Why exactly did you come here?" No more Ozark twang now; he had it under control and sounded almost British upper class.

"I wanted to find out more about Curtis by discovering how he looked through your eyes."

"Why?"

"I need to know the man whose life I'm trying to save."

"You're years too late to save Curtis, Mr. Nudger."

"Probably," Nudger admitted. He liked admitting that less than ever now that he'd met Welborne.

The office receptionist, a tall mannequin-perfect brunette in a tailored brown business suit, swayed into the office, smiled with dazzling whiteness, and sat down behind her desk. Her back was straight and she had the clear, alert gaze of the very efficient. She looked as if she'd been manufactured by I.B.M. and trimmed with lace.

Nudger nodded to her and moved toward the door. "Thanks for your time," he said to Welborne.

Colt looked at him with curiously pained eyes. "I'm sorry I couldn't help you much." His glance shifted to the receptionist, then back to Nudger. "The party in question and I just haven't had much contact."

"You've helped," Nudger assured him. "Blood tells. Peas in a pod and all that."

As he left the office, he heard Welborne in his businesslike pseudo-British accent crisply instructing the receptionist to check the files for this brief or that. Legalese, flowing fast and furious.

Nudger figured the receptionist was in for it today.

13

Nudger had forgotten about the broken lock on his office door. As soon as he entered he knew he wasn't alone; there's something about an occupied room, a slight rise in temperature maybe, or sounds that the conscious mind is unaware of but that register in the subconscious. But as soon as he looked to his left, all of those primal sensors were unnecessary.

A chubby little man wearing pleated slacks and a blue polo shirt was leaning with one arm on the file cabinet. Next to him stood the kind of abnormally skinny but shapely older woman usually glimpsed only in diet-food commercials. She had close-cropped, raggedy blond hair and was wearing an oversized sweatshirt with "Nike" lettered on it, pink shorts, jogging shoes, and was clutching a small, crinkly Gucci purse. She smelled of perspiration and expensive perfume. *Nouveau* jock.

"The guy in the doughnut shop told us it was all right to wait here," the man said. "I'm Charles Siberling. This is my friend Kelly Cole." He paused to kiss her on the cheek, as if that were his way of introducing her to people. "We were on our way somewhere, but I thought I'd drop by to see you first."

Nudger introduced himself, shook hands with both parties, and sat down behind his desk. The swivel chair squealed its hello. Nudger sighed too loudly, as if it felt good to be off his feet. Blond Kelly studied him, then carefully surveyed his humble environs. She returned her attention to Nudger.

"You've hurt your face," she said. Somehow she made it sound like an insult, as if all ugliness were permanent, deserved, and excluded one from the better things in life.

Siberling ignored Nudger's face. "Doreen told me you were trying to get in touch."

"Doreen?" Nudger asked.

"The receptionist at Elbert and Stein. She's an airhead; don't judge the firm by Doreen." He moved over and stood in the mottled stream of brightness from the dirt-streaked window.

Nudger was surprised by how young he looked. His face was sixteen, his eyes about fifty. Average it out and you'd probably have his true age. Blond Kelly appeared to be a well-kept half a century and displayed a certain brand of West End or Ladue snobbery in every line and gesture. The veininess and stretch marks beneath the tan of her legs were like the creases in old folding money. These two people didn't seem to belong with each other; it was as if a computer dating service had decided to play a joke.

"I understand you're interested in the Curtis Colt case," Siberling said. Something flared in the wise eyes, eager points of light, like sharp and brilliant objects glimmering in murky depths. Themselves like the eyes of something dangerous.

"That's right. I've been talking to the witnesses, doing some deeper digging."

"Why?"

"I've been hired to try to establish enough doubt of Colt's guilt to have the execution stayed."

Siberling laughed and shook his head. He had pudgy features and a halo of sandy, curly hair; no one looked less like a cutthroat lawyer. "That's crazy. Colt's exhausted virtually all appeals. Nothing can save him."

"Would the state execute him even if irrefutable proof were put forth that he was innocent?"

Siberling thought about that and laughed again, this time with a bit more humor. "No. Politically it would be impossible, even though legally the execution should be carried out as scheduled. And the state doesn't want to kill an innocent man, Nudger. Especially one who might not stay in his grave."

Nudger leaned back in his squealing chair. The motion brought a jolt of pain around his damaged rib. The pain angled all the way up to his armpit. He sat forward slowly. "Eeeasy," the chair said, like a concerned old pal. Nudger said, "It's possible Curtis Colt was in another part of town when the shooting occurred."

Kelly looked bored, then whispered to Siberling, loud enough for Nudger to hear. "We'd better get going if we're going to get a court."

"Are you a lawyer, too?" Nudger asked her.

She wasn't one for puns. "I mean *tennis* court," she said seriously, almost angrily.

"You have to *prove* the possible in a court of law," Siberling said. "I already busted my gut trying to do that for Curtis Colt."

Nudger wondered what a sharp and fiery young guy like Siberling was doing with Kelly. "Love," he muttered.

"That's a zero score in tennis," Kelly observed. Maybe she *was* a punster.

"I can't prove it," Nudger told Siberling.

Kelly looked confused. "I'm going downstairs to wait," she said. "The doughnut shop's air-conditioned, anyway."

"Oh, sorry," Nudger said, and reached back and switched on the window unit behind the desk.

But even as it began its comforting hum, Kelly was heading for the door and a lower, cooler clime.

"Try a Dunker Delite," Nudger advised her.

Siberling grinned. "She's an odd piece. Married to a judge. I put up with her because she gives good head."

"Reason enough, I guess," Nudger said, trying to figure out Siberling, remembering what Hammersmith had said about the young lawyer being such an aggravation, about how he could sense and exploit weakness.

"You're thinking I'm an asshole, Nudger, and maybe you're right. In fact, you are right; I'm nasty. Maybe because of that I'm also a hell of a lawyer; I fight for my clients. And not just the clients who can pay. I fought hard for Curtis Colt, but there was nothing to use on a jury. The prosecution held every card, and Colt himself wouldn't cooperate. He sat there dummied up as if he hadn't a chance of getting convicted. The proceedings might have been happening on another planet, for all he seemed to care."

"Why would he be like that?"

Siberling shrugged. "It's not unusual. Maybe he was in mild shock; getting arrested and tried for murder is traumatic. I never really got close enough to him to find out what made him so god-damned stoic." Pacing slowly, the young lawyer shook his head. "Yet there was something about him. Maybe it was his stoicism I came to admire. The bastard had a kind of yokel nobility about him, as if he were above everything going on around him in court, people deciding minor matters such as whether he was going to die. You can't help but kind of admire somebody who spits in the law's eye with calm and quiet style."

"I thought lawyers had respect for the law."

"Hah! I respect people, Nudger. And after that I respect the coin of the realm."

"You've got them in the right order," Nudger said. Siberling grinned. "Yeah, but I get them mixed up sometimes." The dull pain in Nudger's side was causing his stomach to act up. He slid open the flat middle desk drawer and got out a roll of antacid tablets, popped two of the white disks into his mouth, and chewed.

"Bad stomach?" Siberling asked. Nudger nodded. "Tension makes it turn mean." He put the tablets away and closed the drawer. "I want to talk with Curtis Colt," he said, "as soon as possible."

Siberling scratched his baby-fat, dimpled chin. "I'm not sure—"

"That you can get me in to see him?" Nudger interrupted. "Or that you will?"

"Ease up," Siberling said. "Chew another one of those white

tablets. I'm Colt's lawyer. I can see him anytime he agrees to see me. And I can send you as my representative.''

"And will you?"

"I didn't say I wouldn't. But I don't want you to give Colt false hope. He's probably adjusted to the idea of the execution by now; he might cling to whatever you tell him and be worse off after your visit. He's been nailed tight for this one, Nudger; he's going to die and you shouldn't tell him otherwise.''

"I won't."

"Who hired you?" Siberling asked.

"Colt's fiancée."

He rolled his eyes. "And she told you Colt was in bed balling her the night of the murder?''

"No, but she had someone who was with Colt at the time of the killing talk to me.''

"Who?"

"Colt's accomplice. They were miles away, in North County casing a service station, when the liquor-store holdup occurred.''

"So you've got the word of a fiancée, and the word of a felon. You call that promising? And where the fuck were these people during the trial? I could have used them—not that it would have helped much.''

"The accomplice is still at large," Nudger said. "I don't know where. He would have had to incriminate himself if he'd testified, risked the chair along with Curtis. And Curtis wouldn't let the fiancée testify, didn't want the police to know about her.''

Siberling made a spreading, helpless gesture with his manicured hands. A glittering gold pinky ring winked out the message that he didn't come cheap; this Legal Aid service was strictly temporary and Colt had been defended by one of the best. "Colt might have had the right idea; the police would have bugged the shit out of her if they'd known about her. And I told you Colt was the noble type, just the sort to clam up to protect his lady love.'' Siberling did

some more pacing, theatrically, as if a jury might be watching.
"I'll try to get you an interview with Curtis," he said.

Nudger thanked him, and Siberling started toward the door and
Kelly and his tennis match. Probably indoor tennis, considering
the heat.

"I got the impression you were a difficult man to see," Nudger
said. "What made you take the time to come here?"

The nasty little man turned at the door and smiled an absolutely
angelic smile. "You want to hear me say it, don't you?"

"I need to hear somebody other than my client and a career
holdup man say it," Nudger told him.

"Okay," Siberling said, "I actually think Colt is innocent.
Don't ask me for sound reasons; if I had any, I'd have brought
them up in court. A good lawyer senses almost as much as he can
prove, Nudger. When it comes to push and shove, life and death,
instinct is king over reason. And all my instincts tell me Colt shot
nobody."

Nudger didn't say anything.

"Better get your locks fixed," Siberling cautioned as he went
out the door.

For a long time Nudger sat silently at his desk. He wasn't sure if
he really liked what Siberling had just said about the Colt trial. It
even crossed his mind that Siberling might in some way be using
him, might have known that simply coming here would shift a
critical balance.

The fiancée thought Colt was innocent and the state was going
to give the wrong man the ride on the lightning. The petty holdup
man thought the same thing. The lawyer was of the same mind.

Now Nudger agreed with them.

He wondered how they would all feel Saturday. And if he
should expect another violent visit from the big man who could
dish it out so well he probably never had to take it. Nudger thought
about how it would feel to have all of his ribs cracked. How it
would be when it was happening, and then later.

Pain wasn't for him. He picked up the phone and punched out the number of the locksmith down the street.

14

Siberling had moved fast. He phoned Nudger the night of their conversation in Nudger's office and told him the interview with Curtis Colt had been arranged.

Nudger was up early the next morning and on the road to Jefferson City. It took him a little over two hours to drive there, first on Highway 70, then south on 54, through the flat, green, and baking heartland of summertime Missouri.

It wasn't the most scenic route in the state. Farmland and open fields flanked the highway for miles, broken only by distant, lonely houses and outbuildings, cedar-post fences, grazing livestock, and sometimes equally placed rolls of hay, like huge pillows of shredded-wheat cereal, distributed by mechanized bailers.

Nudger didn't bother stopping for breakfast or to freshen up when he reached Jefferson City; he drove straight to the ancient and oppressive penitentiary.

The Missouri State Penitentiary was said to contain one of the worst death rows in the country, infested with roaches and flies, plagued by inadequate plumbing and unsuitable medical facilities. After an inmate had served enough time there, the waiting became the revenge and the punishment, and the execution the escape.

The room they left Nudger in was pale green, darker green around the lower half. It was divided by a wall containing a bank of phones. Before each phone was a thick window crisscrossed with wire mesh between the layers of glass. On the other side of this glass were corresponding phones, black, without dials, buffed and scarred and with a dull patina caused by perspiration and long use.

There were no other visitors at this hour. Nudger was alone as he sat before one of the phones and waited. On the metal counter below the phone he saw the usual graffiti—names, phone numbers, occasional profanity, obscure symbols—done in pencil or ink. Over it all someone had used lipstick to draw a perfectly shaped heart. There was nothing written inside the heart, as if whoever had drawn it loved someone but wasn't sure who—or maybe simply wanted to love someone. Nudger touched the tip of the heart with his finger, rubbed, examined his fingertip. It was unstained; the heart was indelible.

Through the glass he saw a door open on the other side of the room. A heavyset uniformed guard entered and moved off to the side. The dividing wall and the glass were so thick that no sound from over there reached Nudger's ears. He saw but didn't hear Curtis Colt enter the room, followed by another armed guard. It was like watching a silent movie.

Colt appeared even smaller than Nudger had imagined him. He was wearing drab prison clothes, and he carried himself stiffly, with a suggestion of disorientation, as if he'd just been awakened from a sound sleep. His dark, down-turned mustache looked the same as in his photographs. His hair was shorter but unevenly shorn, making him appear younger. He seemed at ease as the other guard locked the door, moved to the side opposite his counterpart, and took up a stolid, silent position, waiting for the interview to be over so they could lead Colt back to his cell. All routine.

Colt glanced along the rows of phones and windows, saw Nudger, and moved toward the chair and phone on the other side of the window. When he got close, he squinted hard through the glass, as if fixing Nudger's face in his mind.

Nudger studied Colt as he sat down. There was no longer much defiance in his carriage or manner. At the same time there was no sign of submission. It was as Siberling had said; the impression Colt gave was that the material world was a transient condition beneath his concern. Some truth to that, considering Colt's projected brief future.

Nudger also saw the quiet dignity Siberling had mentioned. Sometimes impending death lent people a sort of solemn nobility, the calmness and insight gained by the acceptance of mortality. But then Colt apparently had possessed that before his death sentence.

Both men lifted the phones' receivers before them at the same time; the black earpiece was hard and cool against Nudger's ear. The phone gave off the impersonal chemical scent of plastic.

"Siberling didn't tell me what you want," Colt said. His voice was calm; it flaunted the Ozark twang that brother Welborne had worked so hard to eliminate. "Said who you was, what it was about, but not what you want."

"I'm going over the old ground in your case," Nudger said into the phone, watching Colt react to his words on the other side of the thick glass. It was as if Colt were halfway dead already, at a sad way station where he might still communicate awkwardly with the living, but didn't really want to. "I'm talking to the eyewitnesses, trying to see how they could be mistaken about placing you at the scene of the liquor-store robbery and killing."

Colt gave Nudger a level look through the window. His lips moved, right there a few feet in front of Nudger, but Nudger heard only the electronic simulation of his voice in the phone. "Why you doing that?"

"Candy Ann hired me to help you."

There was a pause. Then Nudger saw Colt's lips move again, seemed to hear the word half a second out of synchronization. "Who?"

Colt hadn't understood. "Candy Ann Adams."

"I don't know any Candy Ann Adams."

Nudger felt the air go out of him. He settled down farther into his hard chair in surprise, needing contact with something solid, real. This he hadn't expected.

"Your fiancée," he said numbly.

"I ain't got no fiancée," Colt said quietly. Too quietly.

"I know what really happened," Nudger said, pressing on. "Candy Ann arranged for Tom to talk with me. He told me the two of you were in North County, laying the groundwork for a service-station stickup, at the time of the liquor-store killing."

"And you believe that?" There was a touch of incredulity in Colt's voice.

Nudger nodded.

"Sorry," Colt said, "I don't know any Tom. The stickup and shooting went down just like them witnesses said in court. I did wrong, and I'm man enough to take my punishment, no matter what it is."

"I think you're innocent," Nudger persisted. "Candy Ann thinks so too. And so does Siberling."

"My lawyer's paid to think I'm innocent," Colt said logically. "Candy Ann is somebody I don't know. If you think I'm innocent, Nudger, and you're trying to do something about it, believe me, you're pissing into the wind. I'm guilty, man. It's settled. I'm settled."

"Don't be crazy. You've got to take what chance you have."

Colt smiled thin enough to cut paper. "I'm all out of chances. Don't feel sorry for me; the food ain't bad here, and a guy don't have to worry about putting on weight." Brave talk, only half-sincere, holding back reality.

Nudger felt frustration growing in him, digging claws into his stomach. "Is that what's bothering you? You don't want anybody feeling sorry for you because it's bad for your tough-guy image? This isn't a beer commercial or an old Cagney movie. My God, man, you're on Death Row! It's time to give yourself any opportunity, no matter how long the odds."

A flush of anger crossed Colt's face, then was gone. "You don't think I know I'm on Death Row? Listen . . ." But he let his voice trail off, as if reconsidering what he was about to say, deciding against it.

"I know where I am, Nudger," was all he said calmly into the phone. Another expression came and went almost instantly on his dark features. It startled Nudger; for a moment he thought Colt might begin to cry. But his composure was back as quickly as it had slipped and revealed the terror behind it. The emptiness. He needed somebody just then. Desperately.

He said softly, "How is she?"

"All right," Nudger told him. "Concerned about you. That's why she hired me."

"Lucky in love, unlucky in crime," Colt said with a tilted grin. "That's me."

"Right both times," Nudger said. He watched Colt through the glass, letting him think about Candy Ann.

Nudger's stomach began to bother him more now. It growled, letting him know that this conversation with Colt represented stress. He absently fed himself a couple of antacid tablets, chomped and swallowed.

After a minute he said, "Curtis, I think you should give them Tom. It will mean prison for both of you. But this way it's death for you and freedom for him. Freedom until he gets collared for some other job. He smells like a loser. Think about it. Don't let some half-ass code of honor put you in the electric chair."

"I don't know any Tom," Colt said. "And there ain't no honor among us thieves, and surely none among us murderers. Ask any of the guards here."

"You didn't know any Candy Ann, either."

Colt stood up. There was time left in the fifteen minutes they'd been granted for the interview, but he was about finished talking. "I don't know any Tom," he repeated.

And he probably really couldn't tell the police where to look for him, Nudger thought. Tom knew the score and the moves, and he had the fear in him. He'd find a deep hole and cover himself, make himself virtually impossible to find until after Saturday.

"Tell Candy Ann to forget about me," Colt said in a voice as hard as his carved features. "Tell her I'm already dead and to quit poking around in my ashes. I'm dead, and Saturday I'll sit down and then I'll lay down, and she'll know I'm dead then the way I know it now."

He hung up the phone and didn't look at Nudger as he turned and walked to the door. He paused, standing loosely, his hands at his sides.

One of the guards unlocked the door, swung it open, and they escorted him out. The guards didn't look at Nudger, either. He was just another visitor from the world on the other side of the glass. Unimportant. Didn't really belong.

That was fine with Nudger. He got out of there.

15

The drive back to St. Louis was during late morning and early afternoon, when the sun was higher and hotter. The Volkswagen didn't have air-conditioning, and Nudger drove with the windows open, his hands slippery with sweat on the steering wheel, the air pressure from the wind pounding like a drum in the back of the car.

He stopped once, for lunch, at a roadside diner, a place of sun-faded curtains, Formica, and dead flies on the window ledge by his booth. The waitress said she couldn't serve omelets after ten o'clock, so Nudger had a ham sandwich and a glass of milk. His stomach objected, not only to the spicy ham but to the entire distressing day, and five miles down the highway he was chain-chewing antacid tablets.

When he reached the city he drove directly to his apartment, then phoned Danny to see if anyone had been by his office. No one had. He then called Kalas Construction and was told that Randy Gantner was on vacation as of last Monday and wouldn't be back to work until next week. Nudger said he was Gantner's brother from out of town and he had to get in touch with Randy as soon as possible. The girl on the phone said she was instructed not to give out employee's addresses or phone numbers under any circumstances. Sorry, there were no exceptions. She didn't sound sorry, just disinterested.

Nudger replaced the receiver and looked up Gantner's address in the phone directory. He wasn't a detective for nothing.

A shower, a cold beer, and a half hour later Nudger was ringing Randy Gantner's doorbell.

Gantner lived in Bridgeton at the Fox and Hounds apartment complex, an adult singles development of low, tan-brick, modern units built in a U-shape around a swimming pool. Nudger figured Gantner was home. A blue Toyota pickup truck he remembered from the Interstate 70 construction site was parked in front of Gantner's apartment. There was an empty rack for a shotgun in the truck's back window, and several empty beer cans and a broken shovel lay in the rusted metal bed.

The Fox and Hounds was near Lambert International Airport, below the flight pattern. As Nudger stood waiting for Gantner to come to the door, a red-trimmed TWA jetliner roared over low enough for him to glimpse the passengers inside the row of windows. The blast of sound was so great that the water in the pool seemed to shimmer. The three bikini-clad tenants lounging near the diving board didn't look up.

". . . want?" Gantner was saying.

The door had opened and Nudger hadn't heard it. He hadn't seen it because his gaze had snagged on a tall blonde sunbathing on her stomach with her bikini strap unfastened so she wouldn't have a pale stripe across her back.

"I need to talk with you again about Curtis Colt," Nudger said.

Gantner had recently showered, or maybe come in from the pool. His reddish hair was glistening wet and combed straight back. He was wearing white slacks, beaded leather Mexican sandals, and a yellow short-sleeved shirt that laced rather than buttoned up the front. It was laced only halfway, to reveal the hair on his chest and a gold chain from which dangled what appeared to be a large gleaming tooth from some sort of animal. The neckwear went well with the gold stud in his left earlobe. He thought he was trendy, didn't know he looked like a pirate lost in time.

He seemed annoyed, but he shrugged and then stepped back to admit Nudger.

The apartment was small and garishly furnished. Above a vinyl modern sofa hung a mass-produced oil painting of an old three-masted sailing ship forging ahead in the throes of a furious storm on a luminous sea. Paint-by-numbers on a heroic scale. A poster of a cat about to flush itself down a toilet bowl hung on the opposite wall, above the legend "You think your day was rough?" Below the poster was a bookcase that held an expensive set of stereo components. MTV was playing on the big color TV, Mick Jagger strutting his stuff while his voice blasted from the two large speakers on either side of the bookcase. Nudger hadn't heard the music outside because of the aircraft noise.

Gantner ambled over and switched off the TV, a middle-aged adolescent in his Fox and Hounds lair. What the hell, Jagger was a few years older than he was.

"Have you thought any more about the liquor-store shooting?" Nudger asked in the sudden, silent absence of Jagger and the Stones.

"Nothing to think about," Gantner said, standing with his hands in the pockets of his white slacks, "except that in just a few days justice is gonna be done."

"It won't be justice if Colt's innocent."

"There isn't any chance of that, Nudger. I sat in that courtroom. I know."

There was a splashing sound from outside; someone had used the diving board. Nudger looked out the wide picture window and saw that the blond sunbather and her companions hadn't moved.

"Somethin', ain't it?" Gantner said, grinning. He absently scratched his bare chest above the animal tooth.

"Something," Nudger agreed.

"Pussy heaven here. This place cost plenty in rent, but it's worth it. Score, score, score."

"Only once a month," Nudger said.

Gantner scowled like Errol Flynn in *Captain Blood*. "What's only once a month?"

"The rent," Nudger said quickly. "I meant the rent."

"The blonde's an airline stewardess," Gantner said. "Place is full of 'em. They're damn near automatic lays."

The Flight Attendants' Union would have disagreed with Gantner, but Nudger decided to let him fantasize. He imagined Candy Ann walking in here to talk to Gantner, the fly seeking the spider. The spider probably couldn't believe his luck.

"Candy Ann Adams tells me you've been to see her where she works," Nudger said.

Gantner studied him, sized him up, seemed to turn slightly hostile. "So what? You got a claim on that?"

"Curtis Colt does."

Gantner laughed. It was an ugly laugh that revealed silver fillings toward the back of his perfectly even white teeth. "Colt ain't got a claim on anything except his reservation in the hot seat Saturday. A woman like Candy Ann has gotta go on living. I'm just the guy to help her do that."

"She came to you for help."

"And I'd like to help her. My way."

"I think you should know Curtis has a brother," Nudger said.

"He's fond of Candy Ann, and he's mentally slow and simple, maybe dangerous when it comes to Curtis' woman."

"Am I supposed to be scared?"

"You're supposed to be warned."

"What if Candy Ann wants me to come around?" Gantner said, smiling lewdly. "After all, she's the one who approached me. Maybe she ain't ready to be a nun and has her personal needs."

"You'd be smart to stay away from her," Nudger said.

Gantner laughed again. He glanced out through the wide window at the tanned female flesh around the pool. "Don't worry," he said. "Candy Ann ain't all that ripe yet, and there's plenty of good hunting in this part of the woods. The brother can have her."

"You don't say that as if you mean it," Nudger told him.

Gantner motioned with a beefy arm and hand. "Look out there at the pool and you'll see why I mean what I say."

Nudger didn't look outside. He knew he was wasting his time, but he said anyway, "Think about Curtis Colt, and if anything new occurs to you, give me a call."

"Sure, you can *count* on it," Gantner said, telling Nudger what he wanted to hear but laying on the irony. Mocking bastard.

Nudger went to the door and paused. "Don't wear yourself out on your vacation," he said.

"Why not? That's what vacations are for."

"Are you going to travel anywhere? Disney World? The Truman Library?"

Gantner shook his head slowly, his thin lips almost smiling. "Nope, I'm gonna stay around town." His eyes darted in the direction of a loud splash and then back. "Do my special kind of relaxing right here."

"Good. Maybe we can talk again if something comes up about Curtis Colt."

"That ain't at all likely," Gantner said. "It's a shame they don't televise executions. You think they will someday?"

"Someday soon, probably," Nudger said, and opened the door,

catching the sharp scent of chlorine from the pool. He went out into the bright, hot afternoon.

As he walked back to his car he saw that the blond stewardess had refastened her bikini strap and rolled onto her back. She was wearing oversized dark sunglasses and a bored expression. Nudger doubted she'd ever been inside Gantner's apartment.

Nudger drove to his office, thinking that Candy Ann was right about how the nearer the execution date loomed, the harder the witnesses would cling to their stories. They needed to be right about what they'd seen, or they themselves would be guilty of taking the life of an innocent man. Even in the face of the compelling new evidence Nudger hoped for, it might be impossible to get the witnesses to change their stories, to admit that they might have been mistaken as they mimicked their god and dictated premature death.

Not only was Gantner not going to reconsider what he'd seen the night of the murder, he was unmistakably enjoying Curtis Colt's predicament. There were undertones to Gantner's enjoyment that bothered Nudger; the expression on the construction worker's face when he talked about Colt's execution was reminiscent of the faces of children from Nudger's past as they bent studiously to watch a colony of ants slowly devour a writhing caterpillar. What they seemed to enjoy most about the caterpillar's struggle was that there was no doubt about the outcome, probably not even in the caterpillar.

Maybe that was something Colt understood. Though he'd been on the other side of the city from the holdup and murder, that didn't seem to make much difference to him. He had no doubt of the outcome of his life. Like most career criminals, Colt had a soured and cynical view of society. That he hadn't committed this particular crime wouldn't seem to make much difference, not if the cards were marked against him from the day he was born. Sooner or later he had to play a hand and lose everything. The game, his life, was fixed. He was sitting in his cell, certain now, as he had been from the beginning, that he was doomed to be society's victim. Now he was stubbornly refusing to plead, to beg. He wanted to withhold from his antagonists the one thing they were never able to take from him: his dignity.

Nudger called Iris Langeneckert and she refused to talk with him again. She said she had nothing to add, and that she was still certain of her story. Then she told Nudger she would pray for Curtis Colt's soul. Nudger believed her; she was one witness who wasn't taking the consequences of her testimony lightly.

Edna Fine agreed to see Nudger. He drove to her apartment building and parked across the street on Gravois, just down the block from the liquor store that had been the scene of the murder.

It was early evening now and had cooled down to the low eighties. In the west Nudger could see bursts of illumination flashing along the horizon. Chain lightning, it was called, an electrical disturbance that had nothing to do with rain and wasn't accompanied by thunder. It was often visible in the dry, warm evenings of long midwestern heat waves.

Nudger was crossing the street toward Edna Fine's apartment when he saw the blue Toyota pickup. It pulled away from the curb down the block, heading toward him.

Then it braked, made a slow U-turn, and drove away in the opposite direction, west toward the lightning. It hadn't gotten near enough for Nudger to get a clear view of the driver.

When Edna Fine answered his knock she was wearing a dark bathrobe that seemed oddly judicial. Or maybe that was just Nudger's warped perspective. Her hair was mussed and she was holding a long tortoiseshell comb. There were several strands of hair caught in the comb.

"I'm getting dressed to go out," she explained. "An appointment I forgot about. I'm rather in a hurry, Mr. Nudger."

"I won't keep you," Nudger said. "Did Randy Gantner just leave here?"

"Who?" She puckered her old-maid lips in puzzlement.

"Gantner. He's another of the witnesses in the Curtis Colt trial."

She nodded sternly. "Yes, now I remember the name. No, he hasn't been here. Not ever."

"All right," Nudger said, flashing the old sweet smile. "Can I have five minutes of your time?"

"Of course. Five minutes. I can give you that. But I must warn you, Mr. Nudger, I haven't thought of anything new, and I really can't change my story about the night of the murder. Not in good conscience."

And she didn't change her story. Even Edna Fine seemed to be clinging to her version of the facts for comfort as Saturday drew nearer.

Nudger left her with her cats in her lilac-scented apartment and sat for a while across the street in the parked Volkswagen. He was reasonably sure it was Gantner's truck that he'd seen make the U-turn and drive away. But what was Gantner doing here? He had no reason to watch Edna Fine's apartment. And he hadn't gone inside. Or had he? Maybe for some reason Edna Fine was lying about not seeing Gantner. Or maybe Gantner had come to talk with her and hadn't had a chance before Nudger drove up and parked across the street from her apartment.

Another possibility gnawed. The prospect of some sort of collusion among the witnesses. Another development, however vague, that pointed to Colt's innocence.

Nudger clenched his fists in frustration. His stomach rumbled. Sometimes it seemed that he was the only one in his world who didn't realize what was going on. No one would tell him because they had other interests, other directions. He was the only one swimming against the current, stroking desperately to reach a destination nobody else cared about. Sometimes, most of the time, his life was lonely.

He started the car. Then he swallowed his frustration and not a little bit of pride and drove toward Claudia's. Some things he had to share, or they might eventually destroy him. He could share them with Claudia.

Their relationship might be frayed right now, but it would hold. She'd understand. When Nudger needed to talk, she always listened. Always.

He geared down the Volkswagen to take a sweeping curve in the road, then picked up speed, heading east. Behind him the mocking lightning danced wildly in the vast darkening sky.

16

Claudia was home. Nudger saw a light in her front windows as he parked across the street from her apartment on Wilmington.

Though dusk had crept into the city, it was still bright enough for some of her neighbors to be out mowing the small lawns in front of their squared-off brick houses or apartment buildings, or to be ritualistically polishing their cars. That was how they wiled away their time in this part of town. There was a Germanic sense of order that ran deep here. South St. Louisans had been known to cut down majestic trees for no reason other than that they didn't want leaves littering their lawns.

It had been one of Nudger's rougher days. He was tired, and he took the two flights of wooden stairs up to Claudia's apartment slowly. He was a bit surprised at the effort the climb required. Each year his legs seemed to weigh more.

The stairwell was still hot from the afternoon, and the open window on the landing did nothing to dispel the heated air or to lessen the mingled cooking smells that seemed to be common to old apartment buildings.

When finally he stood in front of Claudia's door and had his fist drawn back to knock, the door suddenly swung open.

Claudia was dressed to go out. She was wearing her plain navy-blue dress, high-heeled shoes, and a double string of pearls around her neck. Unpretentious. Elegant. He liked her dressed like that. Her eyes widened wildly for an instant, then she stepped back gracefully and smiled.

But too late. He knew.

She'd been expecting someone else.

Nudger walked into the apartment and looked around. There were tracks of roughed-up nap on the carpet from the vacuum sweeper, and everything was exactly in place. Even the magazines on the coffee table were fanned out precisely like a hand of cards, the way they were in a doctor's waiting room in the morning, before the patients messed them up. Nudger hadn't seen Claudia's apartment this neat since right after she'd moved in.

"Were you planning to bring him back here after dinner?" he asked.

"Not dinner," she said, "a concert in the park." She was defying him now, angry. And building on her anger. What right had Nudger to barge into her home and interrogate her, she was thinking, and she was close to saying it.

"Biff Archway?" Nudger asked.

She didn't answer, letting him know with her silence that, whomever she was going out with, it was none of his business. This was her apartment, her life. Her own.

"I thought we were honest with each other," Nudger said. He felt his stomach knotting up, twisting, twisting.

Claudia slapped her hands lightly against her thighs. She was tense, drawn tight, not liking what was going on here any more than Nudger liked it. An ugly scene getting uglier. Only she hadn't forced a confrontation; he had.

"You knew about Biff," she told him.

Nudger looked glumly at her, nodded. True enough.

Claudia swallowed, then breathed out hard through her nose.

"Look, Nudger, I'm going to ask you for something. It's something that isn't going to be easy for you; I realize that."

He waited, then finally asked, "What is it?"

"Understanding," Claudia said simply.

Nudger gave her a to-hell-with-it shrug he didn't feel. "I'll make an effort."

"I do love you," Claudia said. "Or I think I do. Which is why I'm being honest with you. I don't talk about Ralph or the girls much . . . about what happened. But I still think about it too much."

Nudger understood that. Thinking about Ralph just a little was thinking about him too much.

"You helped me when I needed it," Claudia said. "I'm grateful, and I'd be lying if I said that had nothing to do with why I'm fond of you."

"If you're fond of me, why go out with Biff Archway?"

She moved closer, her dark eyes pleading with him to see her point of view. Her lips twitched nervously before she spoke. "After my marriage to Ralph, even though I love you, I feel that to fully regain my identity, my wholeness, I need to see other men. I've felt that way for quite a while, but I didn't say anything about it." She flexed her long-nailed fingers, eventually working them into tight, pale fists.

He stared at her. "What is this? Kick Nudger therapy? Did Doctor Oliver put you up to this?"

"It was my decision."

"Well, I don't agree with it."

A few seconds passed. Something bright seemed to go out of her. She seemed to have made some decision about Nudger, to have withdrawn to a place behind some barrier in her mind where he couldn't hurt her. Then she shrugged as if to say the hell with what *he* thought. She seemed to mean it.

"We had what the books and talk shows call a relationship," Nudger pointed out.

"We still do. Only it's changed somewhat."

"Like the atomic bomb changed Hiroshima somewhat."

She stepped over to stand next to him, rested a hand on his shoulder. He could feel a vibration running through her fingers. She was wearing his favorite perfume. Biff's, too? "Don't feel that way, please!" she said softly. She wanted to come out from where Nudger had forced her.

He moved away from her hand and walked toward the door. She let her arm fall limp. "Nudger!"

"You wouldn't want me here when Biff arrives," he said.

"I asked for understanding," she told him, as if she were disappointed in him.

"Can't give it to you," he said. "I'm feeling too sorry for myself."

"Damn you!" she said, turning unexpectedly angry. "Don't *you* lay a load of guilt on me! Not you, too!"

"Maybe Ralph—"

"What?" she interrupted, furious and afraid. She stood waiting for him to finish what he'd begun to say, close to tears, close to something else. Scary.

"Forget it," Nudger said, and went out the door.

His heart was pumping and his stomach was churning. He didn't feel at all tired going down the stairs.

He sensed that Claudia had followed him out into the hall and was standing above at the railing, watching him leave. That she might shout something after him.

But when he turned at the bottom of the stairs to look up at her, she wasn't there.

17

Nudger didn't feel like going home to his empty apartment and trying to tune out the silence. He didn't want to find out how sorry for himself he could feel.

His side was aching, throbbing with his heartbeat. First he'd been kicked around physically, then he'd taken his licks mentally. Some life. Maybe the TV evangelists were right and he was involved in some sort of celestial test. Maybe boils and locusts were next.

Women were certainly one of his life's tribulations.

No, not women generally. Claudia. She was primarily his woman trouble of the moment. It wasn't wise to generalize about people. About anything. Thinking that way could lead in wrong directions, and to more problems.

Eileen, for instance. Eileen was a problem and a wrong direction in Nudger's life. But she was hardly similar to Claudia.

Eileen was a problem from which he longed to escape, Claudia one he longed to solve. But he sensed that any solution was beyond him for now, and possibly forever. Maybe it had to be that way. Fate. Fate was always jerking around people who loved each other. Fate had a sense of humor that wasn't very nice.

Nudger chewed antacid tablets and drove around the city for a while, down South Grand with it's odd assortment of little shops and struggling businesses, along side streets lined with solid brick flats and houses lived in by solid German families, then west on Chippewa, past the array of cars and people at Ted Drewes' frozen custard stand, along Resurrection Cemetery with its neat rows of flower-decorated graves. Traffic was heavy despite the late hour, and some of the cars had their hoods unlatched the first few inches to prevent boiling radiators in the relentless heat. Summer in the Gateway City. Sizzle, sizzle.

Nudger listened to the Cardinals game on the car radio. The Cards were winning ten to nothing in the fourth inning. He was glad somebody was having a good night; he knew he wasn't. If only the Cardinals' luck would rub off on him and he could win five in a row of something. Anything.

Finally he decided to go to his office and examine his mail, see if he'd won the Publishers' Clearinghouse Sweepstakes.

Relieved to have a sense of direction, however brief and insignificant, he stepped down on the Volkswagen's accelerator and wished other drivers would get out of his way.

When he pulled to the curb in front of his office, a set of headlights swerved in behind him, then brightened as the car parked with its nose to the back bumper of the Volkswagen. Nudger looked in his rearview mirror. Too bright to see anything; like a damned Steven Spielberg movie. He winced from the glare. Whoever was back there didn't turn the car's headlights off, and left the engine running.

Nudger thought about driving away, but maybe there was no need for that. It could be that the car behind him was a police cruiser, and he was about to get a ticket for a burned-out taillight or a faulty muffler. The old Volkswagen provided a wide range of targets for a nit-picking cop.

Then a chill hit him. Maybe whoever was behind him wasn't a cop. Maybe it was—

"Hi, Nudge."

Danny. *Whew!*

He had walked up beside Nudger on the street side. Now he moved over where Nudger could see him better, stooping slightly on creaky legs so Nudger wouldn't have to crane his neck to stare up at him.

"I seen you turn onto Manchester," Danny said. "I been trying to get in touch with you since late this afternoon. Called at Claudia's, but she said you'd left over an hour ago."

Nudger got out of the car, leaned against the warm metal in the bright wash of the headlights, and listened to the idling engine in Danny's Plymouth tick-tick-tick. Heat was rolling out from beneath the Volkswagen, finding its way up Nudger's pant legs and making him uncomfortable. He shifted position but it didn't help.

"That guy that beat you up was back around here today," Danny said. "Him and somebody else."

Nudger felt another thrust of fear. "Did you see him go up to the office?"

"Nope. Both him and the other guy just sat in a rusty old red pickup truck across the street. The big guy was behind the wheel. They sat there for over an hour, talking and looking up at your office window now and then. Twice they drove away, then came back within half an hour or so and parked over there again."

"You said there were two of them. What did the other one look like?"

Danny stepped closer to the car as a bus passed. The bus was moving slowly, heading for downtown, hissing and belching diesel fumes. A black woman in a window seat stared down at Nudger and Danny from behind the glass as if she were touring another world and they aroused her curiosity.

"The other guy was big, too," Danny said. "Hard to tell next to the driver, but I'd guess around six feet, and built plenty stocky. He had red hair and a real deep suntan. Oh, yeah, I can't be sure, but it looked like he was wearing an earring. He turned his head for a moment and the setting sun caught it, made it glint gold."

Randy Gantner. Nudger knew what it meant if Gantner was connected with the strong-arm who'd beaten him. The beating had nothing to do with Cal Smith's phony insurance claim that Benedict wanted investigated. It was impossible now to doubt: Nudger had been methodically bruised in an attempt to persuade him to drop the Curtis Colt case.

Now someone seemed to have decided he needed another round of unfriendly persuasion.

"Something else, Nudge," Danny said. "I drove by your apartment about an hour ago to see if you were there. I didn't see your car parked where you usually leave it, so I knew you weren't home, but I did see the rusty pickup with the two guys in it. They were parked half a block up from your building where they could keep an eye on the entrance."

Nudger's stomach moved; he swallowed a bitter taste that had formed under his tongue. So Gantner and the big man knew where he lived and were serious about finding him tonight. Showdown time. Nudger would make an equally serious effort to avoid that confrontation.

"Thanks, Danny," he said. "I'll sleep in the office tonight; they won't figure I'd come here this late."

"Is there a reason you don't want to phone the law, Nudger?"

Nudger absently massaged his stomach. "I don't know what the law could do. I can't prove anything I'd tell them about the beating. And it's legal to ride around and park here and there in a pickup truck."

Danny dug into his right pants pocket and pulled out a crinkled piece of white paper, a scrap torn from a doughnut sack. He handed the sweat-damp, abused paper to Nudger. "This is the truck's license-plate number."

"Thanks," Nudger said, doubting the worth of the number. The truck probably had stolen plates, or was itself stolen. Otherwise Gantner and the big man would have obscured the plate's numbers. "I'll give it to Hammersmith in the morning."

"You want me to hang around here with you?" Danny offered.

"I don't see any reason for that," Nudger said. "They probably won't come back here this late, and if they do, the light will be off in the office. Will you leave your car parked there and drive mine home tonight? We can switch again in the morning."

"Sure. Good idea, Nudge. That way they'll figure you never showed up here."

Nudger wished he shared Danny's certainty about that. About a lot of things.

"I got a thirty-eight revolver in the doughnut shop, Nudge. Want to borrow it?"

"No. If I used it, somebody might shoot back at me."

Danny reached through the Plymouth's rolled-down window, switched off the engine and headlights, and they exchanged car keys.

Nudger watched the clattering Volkswagen bounce down Manchester and turn the corner, bucking like a one-man horse with a strange rider. Then he went upstairs to his office.

There was enough artificial light from outside for him to see well enough. He left the blinds raised as they had been since morning and tried to stay away from the window. He did switch the air conditioner on low; it protruded high over the narrow gangway, and he figured its hum wouldn't be loud enough to alert anyone down on the street.

After setting the new dead-bolt lock on the door, he crammed a chair under the knob at an angle. Then he picked up the cracked beer stein he kept pencils in and set it delicately on the chair. If anyone tried to get in, the stein would fall and wake Nudger, and maybe he'd have enough time to phone for help or get out the window and scamper down the fire escape.

He dragged the folding cot out of the closet, set it up, and stretched out on it in his underwear, his pants and shoes nearby where he could quickly wrestle into them. It wouldn't be the first time he'd gotten dressed in panic; he'd acquired a certain expertise at it.

An hour passed before he managed to fall asleep. Then he skimmed the surface of wakefulness, hearing faint sounds, thinking about too much too rapidly, caught between dreams and reality. Curtis Colt and Candy Ann and Gantner and his overgrown friend were caught there with him. Gantner was wearing a pirate outfit with a huge gold earring and was about to swat Nudger with a shovel. The big man stood in the background with his muscle-caked arms crossed, Mr. Clean fashion, grinning his wicked grin. A blond nurse was arguing with a doctor over whether some X rays showed a broken rib or a broken heart. Either way, it was serious. Claudia was there somewhere, too. Only Nudger couldn't quite make out what she was doing, or with whom.

In the morning, nothing was any clearer. Nudger awoke blinded by slanted sunlight, his mouth and his mind full of fuzz.

Danny wouldn't arrive to open the doughnut shop until eight o'clock. It was seven-thirty now, and a prudent time for Nudger to leave the office. Gantner and his massive friend might assume he kept early hours.

He called the Third District. Hammersmith was still on the day shift, but he wasn't due in this morning until about nine. The privileges of rank.

Driving Danny's Plymouth, Nudger finally found Hammersmith enjoying those privileges and a huge breakfast at the Webster Grill near his home. Hammersmith seemed surprised to see Nudger walk in the door and motioned for him to sit in the opposite seat of his booth.

"Had breakfast, Nudge?"

"Not yet." Nudger surveyed Hammersmith's plate. Four eggs, bacon, fried potatoes, jellied toast. There were enough calories there to heat a house. Hammersmith hadn't achieved his bulk without trying. Nudger wondered if it was the wear and tear of the job. Some cops drank. Some beat their wives or kicked their dogs. Hammersmith ate.

"Great fare here," Hammersmith said, motioning with his fork and assuming the air of a gourmet.

A young waitress with pinned-back blond hair came over to the booth and Nudger ordered coffee with cream. "Put it on my check," Hammersmith told her.

Nudger wondered if he'd have said that if the order had been for more than coffee. Hammersmith was notorious for dodging restaurant checks. Dining out was a game for him. Now he probably figured Nudger owed him lunch.

Hammersmith forked potatoes into his mouth and shook his head, chewed, swallowed. "Just coffee, huh? No wonder your stomach rumbles like a capped volcano." He downed half of his own coffee. His sharp blue eyes took in the traffic outside on Big Bend, the Plymouth parked at a meter across the street. "How come you're driving Danny's car? Yours in the shop again?"

"I've been in the shop," Nudger said. "A mountain with arms and legs was waiting for me in my office Monday and gave me a beating."

Hammersmith nodded toward Nudger. "That how you got the unflattering marks on your face?"

"It is. But the guy was a pro; he did most of his work on my body. Very efficient work."

Hammersmith paused in lifting a piece of toast. Some of the strawberry jelly slipped off and dropped onto his plate near the eggs. "I noticed you were walking kinda stiff. Much damage?"

"A cracked rib maybe. And bruises inside and out."

"Know who the guy was?"

"No."

Hammersmith shook his head. "Even if you did, unless you had proof, witnesses, there wouldn't be much we could do. Have a word with the guy, maybe, throw a scare into him."

"He'd probably scare whoever you sent to talk to him," Nudger said, thinking that eyewitnesses or the lack of them were causing him a lot of trouble lately. "The real reason I wanted to tell you about this was because of who might have aimed him at me."

Nudger told Hammersmith about the big man trying to warn him off a case, about noticing Randy Gantner's truck near Edna Fine's apartment, about Danny seeing the oversized assailant with Gantner yesterday.

Hammersmith didn't like hearing any of it. He ate slowly while

Nudger talked, as if he were chewing something that might contain a hidden sharp bone.

"It has to be the Curtis Colt case the strong-arm guy was warning me about," Nudger said.

"So it seems, Nudge."

Nudger reached into his shirt pocket and pulled out the slip of paper Danny had given him. He smoothed it out and handed it across the table to Hammersmith. "Danny got the truck's license number when it was parked across the street from my office. I doubt if it will mean much, but it's worth running an owner check on it."

Hammersmith folded the scrap of paper carefully and slid it into his pocket. His usually smooth, evenly florid complexion was mottled, and there were white lines at the corners of his thin lips. "You want protection, Nudge?"

"Sure. Whatever can be spared." He knew that couldn't be much, and his office and apartment weren't actually within city limits.

"I'll call the Maplewood police; they'll have their cars keep an eye on your building, watch for an old pickup truck with this plate number. And a St. Louis Second District car can swing by there now and then; you're only a few blocks outside the Second. I'll pass the word."

The waitress brought Nudger's coffee, set it on the table, then carefully laid the check in a damp spot near Hammersmith.

"Who's trying to scare me away and why?" Nudger asked. "What are they worried about?"

Hammersmith put down his fork. "The Colt case is closed, Nudge. Finished business." But there wasn't much certainty in his voice. The acid of doubt had begun its work.

"I wish for you that were true," Nudger said.

"You talked to Colt in Jeff City," Hammersmith said. "What did you get out of him?"

"He said he was guilty. He seemed sincere."

"The little bastard," Hammersmith said. Nudger didn't know quite what he meant by that, didn't ask.

"Siberling thinks Colt's innocent," Nudger said.

"What would you expect? Siberling is his lawyer."

"And a game one. He's not just talking; he still believes in his client. Really believes."

Hammersmith sipped his coffee and stared out the window at heavy traffic on Big Bend. A tractor-trailer had turned the corner at the post office at a bad angle and was causing a backup at the Stop sign. A bald man in a shiny red Corvette convertible raced his engine. A driver up the block leaned on his horn. Two skinny teenage girls who'd been crossing the street giggled and pretended to direct traffic. Nothing moved.

Hammersmith said, "Christ!" about the traffic or about Curtis Colt.

"You're not eating," Nudger said.

Hammersmith didn't look at him. "I'm not hungry anymore."

Nudger reached over and got a strip of bacon from Hammersmith's plate, ate it, then lifted the check from the puddle of water.

"My treat," he said. He stood up.

Hammersmith nodded, still staring out at the sunbaked street beyond the comfortable dimness of the restaurant, wrestling with a doubt that came too late.

Nudger patted him on the shoulder and left.

Outside, reason had prevailed. Or maybe it had been the threat of imminent violence from harried drivers late for work. The truck that had caused all the traffic problems was half a block away.

Things were moving again. Too fast.

18

Nudger got into Danny's Plymouth, twisted the ignition key, and joined the traffic on Big Bend. He didn't feel like going to his office; better to give Hammersmith time to get to the Third and phone the Maplewood police about protection. He made a right turn off Big Bend onto Shrewsbury, got onto Highway 44, and drove east into the still low, brilliant sun.

Even the lowered visor didn't do much to block the sunlight. Nudger squinted along for a few miles, then exited onto Eighteenth Street, made his way over to Grattan, and found a parking spot across the street from Malcolm Bliss Hospital.

Malcolm Bliss was a state mental hospital, the one where St. Louis police took the violently insane directly from crime scenes. He had taken a few people there himself years ago as a patrol-car cop. A tunnel connected this hospital with the larger state mental hospital on Arsenal, and if the violent needed confinement and treatment of long duration, they were taken through the tunnel to a world most of us only glimpse in dark imagination. During her marriage to Ralph, right after the death of their youngest child, Claudia had gone through that tunnel.

Nudger entered the hospital and went to the point of her departure and return, the office of Dr. Edwin Oliver.

A nurse had told Oliver Nudger was on his way. The office door was open and Oliver was standing up behind his desk when Nudger knocked perfunctorily on the doorjamb and stepped inside. On the desk were a telephone, some stacks of file folders, a coffee mug on a glass coaster, and a twisted-wire sculpture of a man and a woman dancing. The sculpture looked as if it had been fashioned from a coat hanger, and there was a desperate sort of abandon to it; Nudger wondered if it was the work of one of Oliver's patients.

"Good to see you again, Mr. Nudger." Oliver offered his hand to shake. He was fortyish, large and in good shape, with leprechaun features that suited neither his size nor his profession.

Nudger shook the strong dry hand and sat down in a chair in front of the desk. He noticed that Oliver's small, sparse office was painted exactly the same color as the room in which he'd talked with Colt at the state prison. Maybe the state had gotten an incredible buy on green paint. Or maybe Scott Scalla owned stock in a paint company.

"Is this about Claudia?" Oliver asked. He and Nudger had saved her life two years ago. They both had an interest in her, Oliver professional, Nudger personal.

"It is," Nudger said. "Has she been to see you lately?"

"Not for six months, since our regular sessions ended. Is she all right?"

"I think so," Nudger said, "but I'm not sure."

He told Oliver about Claudia and Biff Archway. Oliver listened patiently, his pointy features intense, like a sage creature from Irish folklore. Even his ears were pointed. Occasionally he absently touched a small scab on his smooth chin where he'd nicked himself shaving.

"Did you come here for Claudia or for yourself?" he asked, smiling faintly.

"Send me a bill and you'll find out," Nudger said. He was annoyed by the question. Oliver sensed it and stopped smiling, then put his serious expression back on. He'd urged Nudger to come to him whenever anything extraordinary was going on with Claudia, hadn't he?

He sat silently behind his desk for a while as if he were alone, looking thoughtful and inching this way and that in his swivel chair. Nudger had closed the door when he came in; on the other side of it now were shuffling footsteps in the hall, voices arguing, fading. Someone kept asking, "Why in the hell didn't you? Why didn't you? . . ."

"If she told you she needed to see other men," Oliver said finally, "why don't you believe her?"

"I do believe her," Nudger said. "That's what bothers me."

Oliver stared at him. "And something else?"

Nudger nodded. "I find myself wondering if she's going to come back to me. If she ever really loved me, or if she was simply grateful because I helped save her life, got her back into teaching."

"Maybe she found herself wondering the same things," Oliver said, bending over backward to make Nudger feel better.

"Apparently so. I didn't need you to tell me that."

"Don't get testy, Nudger. Anyway, Claudia does care a great deal for you. I know; I spent hours with her in analysis."

"Then why Biff Archway?"

"You might have put your finger on it a moment ago. She's wondering about her own feelings. Maybe it's a sign her wounds from the past, from her marriage to Ralph, finally are healing. She feels strong enough now to be with other men, but she needs to verify that to herself."

"Why aren't I 'other men'?" Nudger asked.

"You're too familiar. Too available, sympathetic, and reliable." Oliver smiled now and shook his head. "You should clean up your act, Nudger."

"You're a wiseass for a psychiatrist," Nudger said.

"Doubtless I am. But I'm glad you came to me."

"Why? You said this was all a sign that Claudia was traveling toward full recovery."

"I'm glad for *you* that you came," Oliver said. "Because maybe I can put your mind at ease. What Claudia's going through probably is positive, something she needs to do to affirm herself. When it's run its course, she'll most likely return to you. That's not a professional promise, only my imperfect personal prediction. Dear Abby stuff. An opinion from a friend who's seen this pattern before.''

"I only know I hate Biff Archway, and I never met him.''

"That's natural,'' Oliver said cheerfully.

"So are warts,'' Nudger said, "but they're damned hard to get rid of.'' He thanked Oliver and stood up, started to leave, then paused. "There's someone else I'd like to ask you about, if you've got the time.''

"I don't have it, but I'll listen. Psychiatrists always take time to listen about people's friends. They often turn out to be our clients. The people, not the friends.''

"You won't get a client out of this either way,'' Nudger said. "My friend is someone I'm concerned with professionally. Curtis Colt.''

"Colt? The man on Death Row?''

"Yes. I talked to him yesterday. He's resigned to dying Saturday. He doesn't want help, says he's guilty.''

Oliver fingered the scab on his chin again. "Not so unusual. He's made his peace with himself. He's ready to do penance.''

"Only he isn't guilty. I'm sure of it.''

Oliver placed his hands on the desk, studied them. "Is he your client?''

"No. My client is someone close to him.'' Nudger told him about Candy Ann Adams, about Tom and Lester, about Welborne Colt and his billiard-ball theory of predestination.

"Tell me everything you can remember about your visit with Curtis Colt,'' Oliver said.

Nudger did, while Oliver sat picking at his scab again, causing it to bleed by the time Nudger was finished.

"Colt seems to feel that this execution was scheduled from the time of his birth,'' Nudger said. "That society has it in for him, rather than vice versa.''

"At the same time,'' Oliver said, "his behavior isn't really consistent with that of someone who feels resignation in the clutches of a power with which he can't cope. From what you say, he's accepted the fact of the execution, yet he still displays a calm air of defiance.''

''More one of detachment.''

''But not a dispirited detachment.''

''No,'' Nudger said. ''He acts more like a prisoner of war ready to meet the firing squad as a patriotic gesture.''

''Interesting analogy,'' Oliver said. ''I wish I had the time, and the authority, to find out more.''

''Colt's the one without the time,'' Nudger said.

Oliver nodded agreement. ''If you need to talk to me again about Claudia,'' he said, ''you know how to reach me, here or at my other number.''

Nudger thanked Oliver again and left.

Out on the sidewalk, the sun was much brighter, hotter. The simmering heat wave was going to continue, but right now Nudger didn't mind. He was always glad to leave Malcolm Bliss. It occurred to him that sometimes he had the feeling it was the pocket and he was a billiard ball.

When he got near his office, he saw a Maplewood police car parked up the street toward the Kmart store. A rusty pickup truck was nowhere in sight. Good.

Nudger exchanged car keys with Danny in the doughnut shop. ''Any sign of our violent friends?'' he asked.

''Nope,'' Danny said. ''And a police car's been back and forth by here real slow a few times.''

Nudger told him about the protection Hammersmith had arranged. Not an army of guards, but the best that could be done under the circumstances of short manpower and divided jurisdiction. The St. Louis metropolitan area, with its scores of small municipalities with their separate city governments and police and fire departments, was a puzzle board of official responsibility.

"Call me on the phone if you see the truck again," Nudger said.

Danny nodded and handed him a wrapped Dunker Delite and a large cup of coffee. "Want the morning paper, Nudge?" he asked. "I already read it."

"Sure."

Danny straightened the newspaper as much as possible where it was spread out on the counter, smoothing it and arranging it in order. "Cards won another," he said. "Six in a row now." He folded the crinkled paper in half and handed it over. Newspapers were never quite the same after the first time.

"Thanks, Danny," Nudger said. "For more than breakfast and the paper."

"Nothing," Danny said. "You picked me up from time to time." He snatched his towel from his belt and began wiping down the gleaming counter, working hard on imaginary smudges.

Nudger went upstairs, got his mail from the landing, and switched on the air conditioner.

He sat down behind his desk and examined the mail in the light blasting through the slanted venetian blinds. A couple of ads, a survey form, and an envelope from Eileen. Nothing yet from Publishers' Clearinghouse Sweepstakes. What was the delay? He tossed all of the mail unopened into the wastebasket.

Then he punched "rewind" and "play" on his phone-answering machine.

One message, in a chillingly familiar voice: "You didn't pay no mind to what I told you, Nudger. No mind whatsoever. Start ig-fuckin'-noring that matter we talked about in your office or I'll wring out your balls like an old dishrag. Leave it a-fuckin'-lone, or else. I can be lots more convincing. Fact is, I'd purely love to be."

He reached out a shaky hand and switched off the answering machine. The big guy really liked to mangle things, even the language. He sure sounded like somebody who enjoyed his work.

Nudger stood up and looked out the window at a sharp angle, his forehead pressed against the wooden frame. The Maplewood police car was still parked up the street.

He sat back down, ignored the Dunker Delite, and downed half the cup of coffee. For warmth, not taste. Warmth meant life, and he had the terrible suspicion that he might be heading for a place downtown where the beds had drains and the people were refrigerated.

Such imagination, his stomach growled. Please, no more coffee.

He picked up the phone and called Candy Ann at home.

She was going in early to work at the Right Steer, she said, but she could talk with Nudger during her eleven o'clock break, after the Buckaroo Breakfast Special crowd had thinned out.

Nudger told her he'd be there with spurs on and hung up. He wasn't going to heed the warning of the voice on his answering machine. He didn't know if that was because he was hard to convince, or if he was simply being stupid in a lost cause.

His stomach knew.

19

Nudger and Candy Ann sat hunched toward each other like conspirators in a back booth at the Right Steer. Most of the morning's customers had eaten their fill of ranch-style eggs, steak, and potatoes. The Buckaroo Breakfast Special.

This was the lull between the breakfast and lunch crowds. A few of the other waitresses in their yellow-and-brown cowgirl outfits sat in back booths, looking exhausted and waiting for life to return

to tired legs. Not an easy job, riding herd on customers at the
Right Steer.

"You look worn out," Nudger told Candy Ann. Her gaunt
country-girl face seemed drawn by gravity; her pale blue eyes
gazed out with something like sad bewilderment from beneath
heavy lids.

"I didn't sleep much last night, Mr. Nudger. Ain't slept except
in fits and starts since Curtis was sentenced." She held her mug of
coffee in both hands, sipped from it, then set it on the table exactly
halfway between the two of them, as if it were some sort of magic
potion that would ensure good news. "Have you made any head-
way, Mr. Nudger?"

"No. I'm sorry."

Her thin shoulders lifted momentarily beneath the yellow-
fringed blouse; there was a ketchup stain near her name tag, above
her left breast. "I am, too. Only I ain't in the least sorry I hired
you. People gotta do what they can, don't you think?"

"Some people," Nudger said. He watched a pimply teenage
boy balance two huge bags of hamburger buns over his head and
dance and weave among the tables to the grill area behind the
serving counter. Something sizzled loudly; the place was beginning to fill with that burned-beef smell that didn't agree with
Nudger. "I think there's only one thing left to do," he said.

Candy Ann took another sip of magic coffee, then waited with
her eyes closed, as if hoping the Curtis-saving spell had worked
this time.

"You have to give them Tom," Nudger told her.

She looked down into the steaming cup, then away from it at the
table. "I can't. You don't realize what-all you're asking me to do.
It wouldn't be right for me to let Tom down like that. We got an
agreement. Besides, I couldn't snitch on him even if I wanted. I
don't know where he is." She raised her head and stared at him, a
simple cowgirl trapped in the modern, complicated world and
about to cry. "I mean that, Mr. Nudger."

"Then you can tell the authorities about Tom. Officially. He'll still be at large and as safe as he is now. I think you and I should both make official statements."

"How could we do that?"

"I'll contact Curtis' lawyer and see if we can give depositions. Written sworn testimony. You'll state under oath that Tom exists and that you heard him say that he and Curtis were nowhere near the murder scene the night of the shooting. I'll describe my conversation with Tom. Maybe Siberling can do something with that."

"You really think it might help?"

"No, but it's what we have to do because it's all that's left. And there's a danger for you. The appeal will be a matter of record; the news media will know about it, and Tom might learn that you told the authorities about him. He might try to harm you, to get even."

She thought about that, gnawing her lower lip with her protruding, even teeth. "He might," she agreed. "Curtis told me about some things Tom done. Neither him nor Curtis showed any charitable feelings toward squealers. But with Tom, he seemed to kinda like getting even, according to Curtis."

"I'm only suggesting," Nudger said.

She looked squarely at him. "We'll do it," she said firmly. "When's the best time?"

"I'll try to set it up with Siberling this evening. My understanding is that it's customary for a condemned man to make a final appeal for clemency just before the execution. Maybe in this instance we can make it carry a little weight."

Candy Ann reached over and squeezed Nudger's hand, her own hand still warm from gripping the coffee cup. "Thanks for this, Mr. Nudger."

"Don't thank me," he said tiredly. "The odds are against us. You do understand that?"

She smiled. "Where I come from, most of us are used to long odds. Things often tend to work out for the best."

"You're too optimistic," Nudger told her.

But nothing he could say would knock the smile from that incongruously sexy, American-Gothic face. Blue-sky and waving-wheat faith. People like this had probably homesteaded the West. Nudger understood why the Indians hadn't had a chance.

She smiled wider. "You was the one brought up the idea," she reminded him.

Nudger returned to his office to set things up with Siberling. It was hot, still, and very quiet there. Before he could call the fire-breathing little lawyer at Elbert and Stein, the phone jangled, startling him.

He grabbed the receiver to silence the phone as quickly as possible and give his nervous system a break, then identified himself.

"Hammersmith, Nudge. I thought you might want to know about that license-plate number you gave me this morning."

Hammersmith waited. He loved to dangle information like a prize, make people work for it. Like a kid playing "I Know Something You Don't Know."

"Who owns the truck?" Nudger asked.

"Who knows?" Hammersmith said. He liked to disappoint from time to time, too. It made the times when he did deliver all the more impressive. "The license number won't help you. The plates were stolen from a landscaping company truck out in Richmond Heights, a new Dodge. The rusty job you saw was either stolen or was maybe a junker that's already back in the pile or crushed and on its way to be melted down to make shinier junk in Detroit. Our friends on the other side of the law have been getting their vehicles that way for short-term use. Runners from junkyards, with trash bodies but good engines. 'Junkyard dogs,' some of the blue uniforms have been calling them. Lot of these cars and trucks are from across the river in Illinois, damn near impossible to trace because they don't exist anymore by the time somebody comes around to the scrap pile asking questions."

Nudger hadn't expected much from the license number. Still, he felt almost bitterly disappointed. "Thanks for trying, Jack."

"That's what my wife says."

"Pressures of the job," Nudger told him.

Hammersmith mumbled something unintelligible but no doubt insulting around his cigar, then hung up before Nudger could reply. Another of his favorite games.

Nudger didn't put down the receiver. He depressed the cradle button and punched out the Elbert and Stein number.

Doreen the receptionist was cooperative this time. He had no trouble getting through to Siberling.

Siberling agreed that one last hopeless try to save Colt was in order. A condemned man's attorney had a professional obligation to go to the wire with him, especially if he felt he was innocent. He told Nudger to bring Candy Ann to his office that evening and he'd arrange for witnesses and a stenographer for depositions. The final appeal, with their statements, could be submitted to the governor's office tomorrow, Friday. The day before Colt's execution.

As soon as he hung up on Siberling, the phone rang again. Busy, busy.

It was Edna Fine. She wanted to talk again, to change her story about the robbery and murder. She'd been giving it a lot of thought, she said, not sleeping well since their conversation, and she felt that she had to do this.

Nudger said he'd meet her at her apartment as soon as possible.

As he shrugged into his wrinkled brown sport jacket, he realized he felt better than he had in days. The game might be swinging in his direction at last. Who could say? This was one of those rare and brief periods in his life when he felt a benevolent, fateful wind at his back.

After leaving his office, Nudger ducked into Danny's Donuts, told Danny he might be back late that afternoon, and asked for a Dunker Delite to munch on as he drove. He felt good, all right.

And what Edna Fine had to say might make him feel even better.

He and Candy Ann. Optimists.

20

She hadn't been dead long when Nudger got there.

He saw from the top of the stairs that the door to Edna Fine's apartment was open a few inches, and a heavy dread fell through him, making him walk slower, as if his feet were mired in mud.

When he reached the door he stood motionless in the hall and listened for a moment. The only noise from inside the apartment was a soft and rhythmic sighing sound.

His stomach growled and told him to move one direction or the other. He was in or he was out.

He pushed open the door and stepped inside.

Immediately his gaze fixed on the body. It had been mutilated horribly, beaten, twisted. One of the limbs had been wrenched off by terrible force and lay on the floor near the corner of the sofa.

On the other corner sat Edna Fine. The sound Nudger had heard was her soft and regular sobbing. She held Artemas close to her with almost maternal protection, refusing to look again at the abused corpse of Matilda. Artemas turned his feline head and stared obliquely at Nudger, as if bored by the carnage around him, untouched by Matilda's death. Matilda's yellowish fur was all over the room. A small tuft of it was snagged in the side of Edna Fine's hair, near her ear. Nudger decided not to tell her about it.

What he said was, "Excuse me," and found his way to the bathroom and vomited into the toilet bowl.

After a few minutes he straightened, flushed the toilet, then stood at the washbasin and ran cold water over his wrists. Then he rinsed out his mouth, washed his pallid face, and returned to the living room.

He swallowed several times and tried to ignore the unique and unmistakable odor of fresh blood. He wished he could open a window, but he remembered that they were sealed shut. Breathing shallowly but regularly, he waited for his stomach to adjust and be still.

Edna Fine hadn't moved.

"I was only down in the laundry room about fifteen minutes," she said. "When I came back upstairs, I found . . . this." She looked at the walls, the ceiling, out the window, anywhere but at the mutilated body of her pet on the floor.

"Was your door locked?"

"Yes. I mean, I'm not sure. I think so."

Nudger walked over and examined the door. There were faint scratches on the doorjamb around the latch, as if the lock might have been slipped by plastic or a thin strip of metal. It wouldn't have taken much effort or expertise to get past the apartment's mass-produced and ineffectual lock.

He returned to Edna Fine and rested a hand on her bony shoulder. Was she trembling, or was the unsteadiness in his hand? Nudger always felt helpless, awkward, in the presence of grief. And the intensity of this grief was almost like that of a mother who had lost a child.

"Can I do anything?" he asked. "Get you anything?"

Edna Fine shook her head no. She was sitting motionless now, still hugging Artemas the survivor between her scrawny breasts. Artemas lay coiled in her grip patiently, putting aside feline restlessness for a while, as if sensing that she needed him and granting her a reluctant favor.

"I'll phone the Humane Society," Nudger said.

Edna Fine nodded.

She sat with her eyes closed as Nudger called the Humane Society and arranged for them to drive out and pick up Matilda's remains. When he explained the situation, the woman on the phone said they would have someone there immediately. Animal lovers understood the depth of this grief.

"The Humane Society cremates dead animals," Edna Fine said quietly.

Nudger nodded. "It's the best way."

"Perhaps."

A pet could be a vital factor in the life of a woman like Edna Fine. She was becoming emotionless now, going into mild shock so she could accommodate the vision of what had been waiting for her when she'd walked back into her apartment with her laundry. It would be a long time before the vivid color and savagery of that scene ceased to bedevil her. Sometimes nightmares turn out to be real and irrepressible no matter how much the mind denies them. Somebody had torn apart Matilda in a way that suggested he'd enjoyed it.

"Do you want me to wait here with you?" Nudger asked.

"No. Thanks for offering, though." Still the flat, emotionless voice. She peered myopically at Nudger with her small, reddened eyes. "This is a warning, isn't it?"

"Yes."

"Do you know who did it?"

"I think so. But we could never prove it."

She delicately dabbed at her nose with a knuckle. "I suppose not. That's the way society seems to work these days. People do things to other people who can't prove it. It's like a game the victims don't realize they're playing until it's too late."

"Do you want me to phone the police?"

Now she did look at what was left of her affectionate and trusting Matilda. Edna Fine's long body quaked as if a cold wind had passed over it.

"No," she said, and Nudger knew he'd lost her.

"Has Randy Gantner been here to talk to you?" he asked.

"Yesterday," she said. "He told me you were talking to the witnesses, trying to get them to change their stories. He wanted to know what I'd told you, if I was still sure about what I'd seen."

"What did you tell him?"

"That I was sure. But after he left I began thinking about that night, what I saw from the window."

"Did he borrow your phone?"

Edna Fine looked sharply up at him, startled; Nudger the psychic. "Yes, he did. He said he had to make an important call that couldn't wait. He suggested it was private, so I went into the other room while he talked."

Nudger went to the phone and unscrewed the mouthpiece. He found the bug immediately and removed it, dropped it in his pocket.

"What's that?" Edna Fine asked.

"An electronic device that transmits your telephone conversations. Someone had your phone tapped and knew you called me."

"Randy Gantner?"

"Probably him and others," Nudger said.

"But, why? . . ."

"Somebody—it seems like everybody—wants to be sure Curtis Colt dies Saturday."

"Then Gantner did this to Matilda?"

"Maybe," Nudger said. Or maybe it was the work of the big man who liked to break things, especially if they were alive.

"A warning . . ." Edna Fine repeated, as if finally accepting the reality, a constant terror she must incorporate into her day-to-day living. It was a debilitating apprehension shared by victims of brutality, and by the witnesses and indirect casualties of violence.

"You were going to tell me something about the liquor-store murder," Nudger said, still hoping.

She sat motionless, as if she hadn't heard.

"Edna? . . ."

"I can't, Mr. Nudger." She clutched Artemas to her. "Not now. I really can't." Artemas began to squirm.

Nudger knew Edna Fine would never talk now. Whatever opportunity had existed was gone.

He told her he understood. And he did understand. He knew about the crippling effect of fear that fed on love destroyed. And the monster that had killed and torn Matilda knew about it, too. Had used it to silence Edna Fine.

Nudger didn't say anything else, but he stayed with her until the Humane Society attendant arrived. Then he left as quickly as possible. The presence of violent death, human or animal, sickened and frightened him.

Down on the sidewalk, he forced himself to chew and swallow two antacid tablets. He didn't feel like eating them, but he might be glad later that he had.

He knew that Edna Fine was right. The grotesque thing left on the carpet upstairs was a warning. And one meant not just for her.

21

Nudger picked up Candy Ann at the Right Steer when she got off work that evening, then drove with her through rush-hour traffic to Siberling's Elbert and Stein office in Clayton. He circled the block before finding a parking space on Central, then he fed the meter a quarter and listened to its metallic gurgle as it gulped down the coin like the greedy little civil servant it was.

Clayton was a fashionable near-suburb of St. Louis; Candy Ann, still in her yellow-and-brown waitress outfit, drew stares as Nudger walked with her into the spiffy pale stone building where Elbert and Stein had their offices.

It was still hot outside. The lobby was surprisingly cool, and Candy Ann glanced over at Nudger and managed a tentative smile, as if maybe this wasn't going to be so bad after all. He hoped she was right. The news media would have hold of her when her deposition was made public. That had been explained to her, but still she was willing to do this for Curtis Colt. In fact, once her mind had been made up about giving Siberling a statement, she'd become eager to get it done, get it behind her. Like a trip to a dentist who'd never heard of Novocain.

When the elevator had disgorged a dozen executive types into the lobby, Nudger and Candy Ann stepped inside and sent it zooming back up to the twelfth floor.

The Elbert and Stein offices were plush, carpeted in royal blue with matching ceiling-to-floor draperies. The furniture in the reception room was dark mahogany. Doreen, the balky receptionist, sat at a desk embellished with a vase of long-stemmed roses and a nameplate. She was a heavyset blond woman in her mid-thirties, with a creamy and flawless complexion that was striking in its perfect, fleshy expanse. Probably there wasn't a single imperfection on her entire generous body. She was attractive in a lush sort of way that went with the office.

When Nudger introduced himself, she smiled and said, "Ah, the feisty one."

"Been called worse," Nudger said.

"Bet you have." She stood up. Despite her bulk, her tailored dark business suit fit her well, hung gracefully on her in the way of expensive material. "Mr. Siberling's waiting for you," she said. She shot another wide and beautiful smile at Nudger and led the way. Candy Ann had gotten tentative again. She hung back as they walked down a carpeted hall, and Nudger had to wait for her to catch up.

Doreen ushered them into a large conference room dominated by a long, polished table not quite large enough for Ping-Pong. The royal-blue and mahogany motif had been carried in here, too. Doreen worked a pully device that drew the heavy blue draperies closed, blocking out the slanted bright evening sun, then switched on a brass floor lamp. The net effect, despite the room's size, was a cozy atmosphere; it was the sort of place where secrets were revealed in confidence.

Siberling came in then, along with an elderly woman with gray hair and a bored expression. He was wearing a dark blue pinstripe suit with a vest and carrying a fat leather briefcase. He was all lawyer today. Well, not quite. When he saw Candy Ann, a very unlawyerlike gleam entered his eyes. This was how Caesar had looked at Cleopatra, how Henry VIII had gazed upon leg of lamb.

The woman, who was taller than Siberling, gave a professional nod when he introduced her as Mrs. Kraft. "And you've met Doreen," Siberling said.

Doreen looked wide and pretty and said nothing as Nudger introduced Candy Ann. Siberling was obviously impressed. Nudger thought for an uneasy moment that the cocky little lawyer might actually kiss Candy Ann's hand.

They all sat at the mahogany table, Mrs. Kraft before a gray steno machine that had been set up at one end. Doreen stepped out for a moment and came back with a young paralegal named Jason, who would, along with her, sign as witness to Candy Ann's deposition. Jason was a skinny, acne-cursed kid just into his twenties who looked as if he'd rather be out somewhere with his buddies filling up on junk food.

"You sure all this is gonna help Curtis?" Candy Ann asked nervously.

"I'm sure it might," Siberling said gently, smiling a predator's saccharine grin meant to paralyze his prey. "Only might. I won't make any promises to you I can't keep, Candy Ann. And that's a promise."

Doreen appeared about to be ill, but she said nothing.

Candy Ann smiled back at Siberling and settled into her chair, confident that she had an ally here besides Nudger. The numbers were shifting in her favor. Doreen and Mrs. Kraft were women, therefore natural allies. Young Jason the paralegal was virtually a minor and didn't seem to count. He sat quietly as if that was fine with him, if only he could get out of there soon and watch some MTV.

"Just tell us your story in your own words," Siberling coaxed, "and Mrs. Kraft will record them. Then I'll ask you a few questions. Don't be afraid. Just be truthful. There's never any reason to be afraid of the truth."

Nudger was beginning to understand why Siberling was a good lawyer. If he was too obvious for Doreen, or for most people, his act was working on Candy Ann. And it was Candy Ann he was playing to; he wasn't interested in ratings.

Candy Ann told her story slowly, in a soft voice. About how Curtis hadn't come back to her trailer the night of the liquor-store holdup, and how she'd read in the morning paper that he'd been arrested and charged with murder. She wasn't surprised when she learned Curtis was involved in a robbery. He never went into detail when he told her his business, where he went at night, where the money came from, but she knew. She also knew he wasn't a killer. She knew that gut-deep.

Jason was sitting forward, suddenly interested. This was better than most of the dry, corporate legalese he was used to witnessing. This was maybe even better than whatever he had planned for that night.

The day after the murder, a man named Leonard, whom Candy Ann had seen a few times with Curtis, came to her and told her that Curtis was innocent, and that he wanted her to stay away from the authorities. As far as the law was concerned, she didn't exist, and Curtis wouldn't tell them about her. He wanted her to know he loved her, and he wanted to keep her clean, Leonard had said. How Leonard had gotten this message from Curtis he didn't say. But he knew things about Curtis. And about Candy Ann. The message was for real.

Candy Ann had stayed away from the law, waiting for the trial, then suffering through it and reading about its outcome. After Curtis had been sentenced to death, she didn't know what to do. She searched for Curtis' partner Tom, looked for him so diligently and persistently that finally, probably to keep her from drawing attention to him, Tom came to her.

It was Tom who told her what really happened that night, that Curtis and he had been miles away from the liquor store when the old woman was killed. Curtis had never told her Tom's real name (here Siberling did look dubious, but Candy Ann didn't catch it) and she'd never asked Tom. It was something you didn't ask a man like Tom. Tom was scared; he didn't want to join Curtis on Death Row. So he told Candy Ann to continue to lie low, and that he'd check in with her every once in a while by phone to see how she was doing. Then he gave her some money, half of the loot he and Curtis had accumulated from their night of crime, and went back into hiding.

Candy Ann, knowing Curtis' innocence, couldn't let things lie. She decided to talk to some of the witnesses, who *had* to be wrong about what had happened at the liquor store, to try to get them to reconsider their testimony. But after talking to Randy Gantner, she knew she wouldn't be very effective, so she decided to hire a professional. A private investigator. Nudger.

It was Mr. Nudger, she said, who had talked her into finally telling her story, the true story, in a last attempt to save Curtis' life.

When Candy Ann was finished talking, Siberling leaned back in his chair. He looked thoughtful in the way of a man contemplating a just-dealt poker hand. Nudger could see he was pleased by her statement. It smacked of truth.

"That was fine, hon," Siberling said, reaching across the table and patting her arm.

Doreen looked at Nudger, her expression blank. The young paralegal was gaping at Siberling reverently, as he had been occasionally since he'd entered the conference room. He looked like the

kind of boy Candy Ann should be dating instead of sitting here
taking a desperate chance on the truth about a hard-edged holdup
artist.

Nudger thought Siberling would question Candy Ann exten-
sively, but he didn't. He merely asked some questions that cleared
up any possible language problems in her statement, then questioned her in a way that emphasized pertinent details.

Siberling thanked Candy Ann, who sat back and looked pale and
mentally drained. "You did fine," he told her. "You just relax
now. Can I get you anything to drink?"

She shook her head no, staring down wearily at her hands folded
on the table.

Nudger's turn. He told his story simply and to the point, including his visit with Curtis Colt on Death Row.

When he was finished his throat was dry, but he got no offer of
something to drink.

Siberling nodded to Mrs. Kraft and Jason. Jason smiled nervously, looked long and hard at Candy Ann as if that was what
he'd wanted to do since he walked in there, then left the conference room.

"Mrs. Kraft has an appointment to keep," Siberling said, "but
Doreen can transcribe the statements while we wait. Then the signatures can be notarized. Ordinarily we could take care of most of
that tomorrow, but we don't have time to spare. We have to think
of Curtis."

Candy Ann made big eyes at him and smiled. Thinking of Curtis
was all she'd been doing lately. It was nice to find someone who
shared her obsession.

When Doreen got up to leave with Mrs. Kraft, to begin her
word processing and copying, she surprised Nudger. She smiled
genuinely and brushed her fingertips lightly across Candy Ann's
shoulders in sympathy. Nudger and Siberling exchanged glances;
Candy Ann should have testified, all right.

Siberling excused himself for a few minutes and left the room.

Candy Ann stared across the table at Nudger. The blue draperies and carpet made her eyes seem younger and a deeper blue, almost violet. For an instant she was twelve years old. She looked like a little girl at a kitchen table way too large for her, waiting for vegetables she didn't like but would dutifully eat.

When she spoke, the words caught in her throat. "It keeps going around in my mind, Mr. Nudger, how if they do go ahead and . . . do what they're planning to Curtis, I'll have nobody then."

Nudger didn't know what to say. He mumbled, "Don't you have family?"

She shook her head. "An uncle in Tennessee, but I ain't seen him in over twenty years. I heard he took too much to drink. That's what killed my daddy, drink."

"It's like that in some families," Nudger said.

A faintly puzzled expression pulled at her features. She frowned. "It all didn't seem real until lately. I mean, it didn't seem Curtis was really going to be gone."

Nudger managed what he hoped was a reassuring smile. It felt stiff; if he listened closely, he might hear his face bend. "Maybe he won't be executed. Maybe what we're doing will help."

She let out a long, slow breath. "Lord, I hope so." Nudger didn't think it was merely an expression; it sounded like a prayer from the heart.

Siberling returned with three cups of coffee on a tray with cream and sugar. "It'll be a while," he said, setting the tray on the table near Candy Ann. Steam rose from the cups, visible against the blue draperies.

The three last friends of Curtis Colt sat in the quiet conference room and sipped coffee and waited for Doreen to finish preparing the depositions.

After a little more than an hour had passed, Doreen stuck her head into the conference room and asked to see Candy Ann so she could read and sign the transcript of her statement.

When she'd gone, Siberling poured his fourth cup of coffee and grimaced at the stuff's cumulative bitterness. He glanced at the door Candy Ann had just closed behind her. "Country," he said, "but very nice. Sexy. Nothing like that where Colt's going."

"You really don't have much hope for Colt, do you?" Nudger said.

Siberling had removed his coat. Now he unbuttoned his vest and loosened his tie. "I never told you I did hold out much hope. But the law's unpredictable. It can be twisted like soft putty. So we use the machinery that might just twist it in the right direction, until there's no more fuel to keep the gears turning. We see what happens."

"And when the machinery stops?"

"Someone says, 'Won't you please have a seat, Mr. Colt.'" Siberling smiled humorlessly. "We're among the last civilized nations in the Western world to execute people, but we do it with style: the last meal, the priest, the media's graphic descriptions of the death throes."

"When will we stop it?" Nudger asked.

Siberling looked curiously at him. "I'm not sure if we should."

Nudger stood up and stretched, keeping his silence. He didn't feel like getting into a philosophical discussion on capital punishment. Not with a lawyer. Especially one like Siberling.

Siberling kicked softly at the thick briefcase by his chair. "The last-minute appeal to the governor," he said, sounding as bitter as the coffee tasted. "The fox appealing to the hound."

"And not a hound known for the quality of mercy," Nudger said.

The door opened and Candy Ann came back into the room. She seemed relieved, as if now that she'd signed her name to something, she'd taken a positive step that might lead to Curtis Colt's survival.

"That Miss Doreen wants you to sign your statement," she said to Nudger.

She stepped back out into the hall, as if she didn't want to be alone with Siberling. Maybe she was more observant than she seemed. Siberling followed her.

While she and Siberling watched, Nudger read over his statement and signed it. The witnesses' signatures were already affixed. Doreen was the notary public. She used a bulky silver seal to notarize the signatures, then signed her own name. There. All proper and official.

"I'd suggest we have a drink and talk," Siberling said, tapping the edges of the papers in line, "but I'm going to be working late on this tonight." He touched Candy Ann's slender shoulder with a confident lightness and familiarity, as if she were rare and delicate and only he knew how to handle her. "You just try not to worry, you hear?" Why, he was a little bit country himself, with his libido stirred by Candy Ann.

She nodded, absorbing the sympathy like a sponge with sex appeal. Doreen and Nudger looked silently at each other. Doreen wasn't the airhead Siberling thought, if he really *did* think that.

"Time for us to head for the barn," Nudger said amiably, with just a trace of a drawl, and guided Candy Ann from the office.

As the door swung closed behind them, he heard Siberling say softly to Doreen, "Barn?"

Nudger thought of going back and telling the little lawyer "heading for the barn" was just an expression, country slang for going home. Then he decided to let Siberling live with his imagination.

It wasn't quite dark outside, and it was still hot. A sunset raged like low fire between the buildings to the west. To the east, dusk was settling over the city like lowering, heavy soot from thousands of chimneys. Traffic was thin on Central now, and about every other car had its lights on. The late workers were on their way home from their offices. When the stores closed in a few hours, Clayton would be almost deserted.

"Do you want that drink?" Nudger offered, when he and Candy

Ann had gotten in the Volkswagen. "Don't be ashamed if you need it. What you just did wasn't easy."

She hesitated, then aimed those doll's blue eyes at him and nodded.

"I need it," she said.

22

They'd stopped at the bar of a Hunan restaurant on Brentwood and each had two drinks. Nudger drank beer. Candy Ann sipped at tall Tom Collinses and finished them off with deceptive ease.

At first she'd been silent, pensive. But by the second drink she became talkative. She talked about Curtis Colt and nothing else. Nudger got tired of her trying to wheedle some sort of affirmation out of him that there really was a way to save Curtis from Saturday's appointment with high-voltage death. It hurt him to look into the blue agony of her wide eyes; he wished he could help her, help Curtis Colt, but he couldn't.

When he drove her home and was parked in front of her trailer, she asked if he wanted to come in for another drink. From a more worldly woman Nudger would have suspected the invitation was a come-on, but Candy Ann might only have served him lemonade, maybe with gin in it, and more talk about Curtis.

He declined politely, waited until she was safely inside with a light on, then put the VW into gear and drove down Tranquillity Lane and out of the trailer park.

The night was finally cool. He drove fast with the windows down, listening to the rhythmic boom of air pressure in the back of the car and to some B. B. King blues on the radio.

All that electric-guitar-backed energy blaring from the speaker made Nudger realize he was tired.

Fifteen minutes after he'd let himself into his apartment on Sutton, the phone rang.

It was Harold Benedict. "Nudger," he said, "I need to talk to you about that insurance job."

"Calvin Smith? He of the bad back?"

"That's the one."

"Weren't the photographs okay?"

"Oh, yeah, sure. It's something else. Something altogether different. There might be another hitch in denying the claim."

Benedict sounded not quite himself. "What do you mean?" Nudger asked. "It seemed locked up to me. The guy did everything but an Olympic gymnastic routine right there in his driveway, and you've got it all in graphic detail, in living, incriminating color."

"It isn't the photographs, Nudger. We need to meet and talk about this case. I'm near your place now."

Nudger looked around his unkempt apartment. It needed vacuuming. Needed shoveling. Then he considered how the office looked. He said, "Why don't you come on over?"

"No," Benedict said hastily. "Better if we meet somewhere. I'm at the Steak 'n' Shake restaurant on Manchester. The one in Maplewood. Can you meet me here?"

"In fifteen minutes," Nudger said, and hung up.

Steak 'n' Shake had been on Manchester in Maplewood for as long as Nudger could remember. It was part of a chain that years ago had specialized in curb service to teenagers, a place where they could show off their cars while attractive waitresses in unisex black-and-white uniforms glided over with trays of hamburgers and french fries, then retreated to their station, full well knowing they were being inspected by the customers. Tradition had fallen, and now the restaurant catered to an older crowd and no longer offered curb service.

When Nudger entered through the glass double doors, he saw Benedict seated at a back booth. There were about a dozen other customers scattered around the place, most of them at the counter up front. It was a diverse bunch. There were two bearded bikers in leather jackets at the counter, a young couple with a baby in a front booth, two elderly well-dressed women in another booth, not far from three thirtyish guys quaffing Cokes and wearing service-station shirts with the sleeves rolled up. Over in a corner some teenagers were chewing with their mouths open and giggling. Benedict, short, balding, wearing a white shirt and striped tie, rounded out the group nicely. Or did Nudger round it out, the fortyish guy in the rumpled sport jacket and a day's dusting of whiskers?

Benedict was having chili mac and a Coke. When he peered up at Nudger over the dark rims of his thick glasses, he stopped chewing, swallowed, and stood up halfway. His white paper napkin slid from his lap onto the floor, but he didn't seem to notice. A slight breeze caught it and wrapped it around his ankle, so lightly that he didn't feel it.

They shook hands and Nudger sat down across the table from him.

"This is good stuff," Benedict commented, settling back down and motioning toward the chili mac. He took another generous forkful.

A waitress who walked as if she had an ingrown toenail limped over to the table, and Nudger ordered a vanilla milk shake.

Sore foot or not, it didn't take her long to fill his order. When the shake had arrived, Nudger ate the cherry off the top and asked Benedict what was the problem with the Calvin Smith insurance case.

"Nothing," Benedict said, wiping his mouth with the back of his hand. He took a sip of Coke. "That's not really what I wanted to talk to you about."

Nudger felt a vague uneasiness. He looked out the window, across the street, at a used-car lot that was closed and dark. The dull headlights of the front row of cars stared back dispassionately at him. A few of the chrome grilles were smiling.

"I didn't want to tell you the truth when I called," Benedict said, "because your phone might be tapped."

"Why would anyone want to tap my phone?" Nudger asked, remembering some of his recent conversations with Claudia. Nobody's business, those. Then he remembered that Edna Fine's phone had been tapped.

"I've heard rumors that concern you," Benedict told him, putting down his fork. "You're trying to muck up the works in the Curtis Colt execution."

"That's no rumor," Nudger said. "It's a fact, and no secret."

Benedict waved a smooth hand. A diamond ring picked up the overhead fluorescent light and glinted. "No, no. What I've heard—and don't repeat me—is that someone high in state government is displeased by your enthusiastic pursuit of clemency for Colt."

Nudger sat back, his fingertips caressing the cold curve of the milk-shake glass. The coolness from the damp glass seemed to run up his arm and throughout his body.

"Scott Scalla?" he said.

Benedict shrugged. "I don't know. More likely someone in his administration whose political wagon is hitched to Scalla's rising star." He forked in more chili mac. "Politics, Nudger, make more difference in people's lives than they imagine."

"Someone's been trying to warn me off the case in very physical terms," Nudger said, "completely ignoring Roberts' Rules of Order."

Benedict nodded. "I know."

"The governor," Nudger said, shaking his head, "the governor of Missouri wouldn't hire muscle."

"Probably not," Benedict said wryly, "considering he has the Highway Patrol at his disposal. The thing is, if you do manage to come up with something that delays the execution, that will look bad for Scalla, because Curtis Colt is his project. And if they do go ahead and execute Colt on schedule, and *then* it turns out you've found evidence of his innocence, that's catastrophic for Scalla. He will have personally railroaded an innocent man to his death in order to get elected. There aren't a lot of repeat votes in that.''

''But what if Colt really is innocent?''

''At this point,'' Benedict said, ''that's almost irrelevant to anyone other than Colt.''

''And my client,'' Nudger pointed out.

''Yes,'' Benedict agreed sadly, ''your client.''

Nudger sucked milk shake up through his straw and thought about what Benedict had told him. If it was true, Nudger had gone beyond stirring up hornet nests and had antagonized a den of bears. That was scary. On the other hand, some pieces here didn't quite fit.

''I think one or more of the witnesses is trying to scare me off the case,'' he said. ''One of them, a guy named Gantner, was seen with the strong-arm type who kicked me around my office.''

''Isn't Gantner the witness who works for Kalas Construction?'' Nudger nodded.

''Kalas Construction does a lot of state highway work, Nudger.'' Benedict raised his eyebrows above the dark frames of his glasses.

So there it was, a possible connection between Scalla and Gantner. Possible.

''I want to stress,'' Benedict said, ''that what I've told you is only rumor. A friend of a friend in Jefferson City passed it on. Maybe it's the sort of story that would naturally grow out of the fact that Scalla is so eager to see Colt burn. I don't know. I thought you should be told, though. It might put things in a different light for you.'' He wielded his fork quickly and nimbly and finished off his chili mac.

A different light. Maybe that was the idea. Maybe someone had deliberately started the rumor to scare Nudger away from the Colt case. They would know they could get the story of the state's displeasure to Nudger through Benedict. Nudger did work for Benedict; they were friends of a sort. If someone in Jefferson City wanted to get something like this to Nudger's ear, Benedict would be the perfect conduit.

"Possibly you're being used," Nudger said.

Benedict finished his Coke, making a rattling, slurping noise with the straw. He knew what Nudger meant. "I've thought of that. You could be right. On the other hand, I felt it my duty as a business associate—well, as a friend—to tell you what I heard. It *might* be true, like anything else in this world."

"Anything else?" the waitress asked, startling Nudger. She was standing just behind his left shoulder, leaning close.

"Nothing, thanks," Nudger said. Benedict shook his head no and smiled at her. She left their check on the table and limped away.

Nudger knew Benedict had taken a risk for him. "I appreciate your telling me this," he said. "You *are* a friend. A good one."

Benedict looked momentarily embarrassed. He was used to being accused of maliciousness, deviousness, irrelevance, incompetence, and ambulance chasing; compliments were rare in his line of work. Possibly he didn't like them, maybe even considered them an indication of weakness.

As Benedict reached for the check, Nudger snatched it out from beneath his hand. Benedict, back in character, didn't object.

He and Hammersmith were eating well off Nudger lately.

On the drive back to his apartment, Nudger found himself glancing into his rearview mirror. A large car with a weak, yellowish right headlight stayed close behind him for a while, but continued down Manchester when he made a right turn on Sutton.

What Benedict had said bothered Nudger, about how whether Colt was innocent now mattered only to Colt. It wasn't quite true, but it was true enough to be disturbing. It seemed that justice itself had become irrelevant. Only Candy Ann, Siberling, and Nudger wanted Colt to be innocent.

Nothing else Benedict had said might be true. Possibly it was all rumor, and not even deliberately begun. It might be only coincidence that Randy Gantner worked for a construction company that did state highway work. And not such a coincidence at that; how many big construction companies, or large Missouri companies in whatever business, didn't somewhere along the line do work directly or indirectly for the state?

Still, when Nudger got home, he examined his phone as he had Edna Fine's. He found nothing, but that didn't mean the line wasn't tapped. Or that the apartment wasn't bugged. There were too many spy and pry gizmos in this world for comfort.

He spent an hour carefully searching the apartment for bugs. Benedict's assumption that his phone might be tapped had gotten to him, fanned his frustration and anger.

The going was slow. Nudger wished he had some electronic sweeping equipment to make things easier. Maybe he'd lighten up on his next alimony payment to Eileen and see what Radio Shack had to offer.

Behind the sofa, he found a huge brown spider that threw a strong scare into him.

But that was the only bug he found.

23

In the morning, Nudger read a news account in the *Post-Dispatch* revealing that a "surprise witness" had submitted a statement in the Curtis Colt case. The article went on to explain that Colt's alleged fiancée had known of his whereabouts the night of the murder but had remained silent during the trial for personal reasons. Now she had second thoughts and was trying to save Colt's life. The prosecuting attorney was quoted as saying that this sort of thing wasn't unusual in capital-offense cases; the woman's story, apparently corroborated by a private detective she'd hired, would be dealt with in due legal course.

Nudger set the folded paper down on Danny's counter and snorted in disgust. He knew what "due legal course" meant: Curtis Colt would be executed on time tomorrow morning.

Danny rang up a sale of glazed-to-go for one of the office workers from across the street, then drifted over and brought Nudger's coffee back up to the cup's brim. He gazed at Nudger with his sad hound eyes.

"It ain't going good?" Danny asked.

"Not good at all." Nudger bit into his free doughnut, remembering not to grimace in front of sensitive Danny. He wondered what use the office girls across the street had found for the glazed-to-go they bought faithfully every weekday morning. The doughnuts were too greasy for paperweights, though they were plenty heavy enough for their size. Maybe they used them to play some sort of field hockey in the ladies' room.

"Maybe Colt really is guilty," Danny offered.

"I don't think he is, Danny. And I guess that's the real problem. I started out on this case going through the routine, earning my fee. Then somehow I became a believer."

"You wouldn't believe without reason, Nudge. What about this Candy Ann woman in the paper, what she says?"

"She's telling the truth," Nudger said. "Even her lawyer thinks so. Genuinely thinks so."

Danny looked thoughtful and wiped his hands on the grayish towel tucked in his belt. "I wonder if the prosecutor really thinks Colt's innocent, too."

Nudger had wondered that himself. "Has anyone else been around looking for me?" he asked.

Danny shook his head. "Not lately, Nudge."

"You going to be baking this morning?"

"Nope. I'm overstocked now, especially with jelly doughnuts."

"Keep an eye on the street," Nudger said, "and let me know if anyone starts up to my office."

"Sure. You expecting somebody you don't want to see?"

Nudger thought about that. He was expecting too many people he didn't want to see. That was what his job, his life, had come down to. He sure wished he knew some sort of trade other than the twisted one he worked.

"Probably anybody who'd come by this morning, I'd be better off being warned," he said.

Carrying his coffee, the folded paper, and the weighty uneaten part of his Dunker Delite, he left the doughnut shop and trudged upstairs to his office.

While he was waiting for the window unit to cool the place down, he went in and stood before the basin in the half bath and splashed cold water onto his face. He dried with a rough towel almost as gray as Danny's, then walked to the window and looked down at Manchester Avenue. Nobody was parked across the street, and only the usual number of pedestrians strolled along the sidewalks.

He sat at his desk and went through his mail, ignoring his answering machine. But the phone wouldn't leave him alone. It jangled and Nudger snatched it up, thinking it might be Danny warning him someone was on the stairs.

It was Candy Ann.

"A buncha reporters came out to the Right Steer and wouldn't let me work," she said. "The boss told me go ahead and take the day off, but when I went home more of them was outside the trailer waiting for me. They even had a little TV camera."

"You tell them anything?"

"No. Mr. Siberling told me not to talk to the press without him there."

"Where are you now?"

"I'm in a room at the Ramada Inn out by the airport. Mr. Siberling came by my place and read a statement to the reporters, then he drove me out here without anybody knowing where we was going. So I'd be let alone."

"Are you all right?" Nudger asked.

There was a pause. A muffled roar, as if from a jet aircraft flying directly overhead, came over the phone. "Yeah, I'll be fine."

"Is Siberling there?"

"No, he said he couldn't be. He's still working on the appeal for a stay of execution, he said. He left me here about half an hour ago. It's room Two-twenty."

"Stay there; don't go out except to eat," Nudger told her. That should be safe; there hadn't been time for a photograph of Candy Ann to appear in the papers, and probably she wouldn't be on TV until the evening news. "If anybody from the media does question you, just tell them no comment and go back to your room."

"Okay, Mr. Nudger. It's number Two-twenty."

"You told me that."

"Yeah, I did, didn't I."

"I'll check in with you from time to time today to make sure you're all right," he said.

She thanked him, staying on the line and forcing him to hang up first. He wondered if Scott Scalla knew there was a woman who'd gladly sit on Curtis Colt's lap in the electric chair. Would the governor understand that? He wasn't sure he understood it himself.

The media began showing up intermittently at Nudger's office. He no-commented a feature writer from the *Post*, and did the same to a reporter who phoned from the *Globe*. When the *West County Journal* called, Nudger knew the media might not give up for a while. He sympathized with the news folks. They had their job to do; he just didn't like being their job.

To assuage his conscience, he phoned Ron Elz, a columnist at the *Globe*, and gave him the story, but on the condition it wouldn't appear until the Sunday column. He could trust Elz, who had a high regard for the truth and would print it straight. He was somebody Scalla couldn't get to, if the governor's office actually was involved in trying to intimidate Nudger.

When the *St. Louis Voyeur*, a local tabloid scandal sheet, called, Nudger decided it was time to get out of the office and away from leading questions.

He accomplished this by driving around town and trying to talk to the witnesses again, really making a pest of himself.

Edna Fine was still afraid and grieving over the death of Matilda; Nudger saw that talking to her was hopeless and painful and left her alone. Sanders wasn't home, and according to his boss at Recap City, he was off work and away on vacation. No one else was available to talk with Nudger. He even tried Randy Gantner's apartment at the Fox and Hounds, but he was told by an emaciated blonde at the pool that Gantner hadn't been home for several days and was probably out of town.

Finally Nudger had a late lunch and drove to the Ramada Inn to see how Candy Ann was holding up.

She was alone in 220, looking as if she might have been crying, yet she seemed calm. The room was one of the cheaper ones, but she thought it was palatial. And the soda machine was right down the hall. Free ice and everything.

Nudger brought her some hamburgers from a nearby Hardee's. She devoured them as if she hadn't eaten for years and had just been reminded there was such a thing as food. Then they sat and drank Classic Cokes from the machine. She laced her Cokes with gin. Nudger thought that was a good idea. He listened while she talked about Curtis Colt, and how life had been where she was raised in northwestern Arkansas: rough, nothing like the Waltons' life in reruns on TV. "Rocks," she said. "Arkansas soil don't grow no crop better than rocks. It's a hardscrabble way to live, Mr. Nudger." A way to live that Curtis Colt had rescued her from, and now she was trying to rescue him in return and not doing so well.

It was almost evening when she sat back in her chair and started to doze off. She snored softly and delicately; even that generated sex appeal. He shook her gently and told her he was going.

"There isn't anything more we can do now," he said. "You might as well rest here."

She nodded, staring up at him with wide but sleepy blue eyes. Doll's eyes. A doll in trouble in real life.

"You want me to stay longer?" he asked.

"No," she murmured, "Mr. Siberling's coming here this evening to hope with me."

He would be, Nudger thought. But Candy Ann would be okay. Siberling would lie to her far more plausibly than Nudger could.

Nudger left her sleeping in the chair. Walking quietly, he locked the door carefully behind him.

Watching Candy Ann eat had made him hungry. He stopped for an early supper of Chicken McNuggets and french fries, then drove by his apartment to make sure no one from the news media was lurking about with pen and pad or recorder.

There was no one in sight. Once he managed to get inside, he closed the draperies, opened a can of beer, and settled back to watch a televised Cardinals-Mets game.

By the third inning the score was six to nothing, Cardinals, on their way to winning their seventh game in a row, and Nudger couldn't sit still any longer. His mind was on too many things other than the ball game. He was with Candy Ann in that tiny room at the Ramada Inn. He was with frightened Tom wherever Tom was. And he was with Curtis Colt in his cell on Death Row, waiting for morning and nine o'clock and high voltage.

Nudger knew whom he wanted to be with in reality. He switched off the TV and phoned Claudia.

When she answered, he didn't speak. He was afraid that if he did she'd find some reason for him not to come to her apartment.

He needed her presence, to see and touch her; he'd had enough of disembodied voices on the phone and people half removed from the world or distracted by grief. He didn't want to be alone tonight. Not through the dark hours of waiting. Siberling had told him there wouldn't be an outcome to the final appeal for Curtis Colt's life until morning. After a long, long night for a lot of people.

He hung up the phone and chewed a couple of antacid tablets, even though his stomach felt okay at the moment. Nights had always provided the toughest hours of Nudger's life, both professionally and personally. Crimes of madness and impulse were committed during the long summer days, but here in the simmering city on the Big Muddy, the calculating and the deadly waited for the comparative coolness of nightfall.

His stomach growled softly, as if to say thanks for the precaution. He flicked the rolled-up tinfoil from the antacid tablets into the wastebasket, then he hurried downstairs to where his car was parked behind the building.

24

Claudia's south St. Louis neighbors were passing the summer evening in their usual fashion. The men were outside mowing already mowed lawns or cleaning their cars, while the wives were inside cleaning ovens or going around baseboards with knife points to get all the dirt out. Scrubby Dutch, the predominantly German Catholics and Lutherans in this part of town were often called. It was a traditional, conservative area, maybe the character and backbone of the city, where everyone got along with everyone else as long as nobody marched out of step.

An old gray-haired guy wearing shorts and a sleeveless white undershirt leaned down to buff his Buick's hubcaps and glanced over at Nudger, then looked away. Somebody had the ball game tuned too loud on his radio. Jack Buck and Mike Shannon, the sports announcers whose voices permeated St. Louis summers, were shouting about a great play while the crowd roared.

As Nudger entered the building and climbed the stairs to Claudia's apartment, the nattering of the radio outside faded from his consciousness.

At Claudia's door, he cocked his head to the side and stood still, listening.

A violent thumping sound was coming from inside the apartment, and there were faint voices. And music. Something heavy was striking the floor regularly, hard enough for Nudger to pick up vibrations out in the hall.

He slowly rotated the doorknob and pushed in on the door. There was no give; it was locked. He fished his key from his pocket, inserted it in the lock, and twisted. Then he quietly opened the door a few inches and peered inside.

The first thing he saw was a husky, perspiring man standing with his fists on his hips. He was wearing only sweat-stained red jogging shorts, and he was staring down at the floor, at something out of Nudger's line of sight, grinning with handsome animal savagery. Nudger edged the door open an inch wider and saw the bare feet and legs of a woman lying on the carpet.

He threw the door full open and stepped inside, hearing the knob crack a chunk of plaster out of the wall.

"Nudger!" Claudia said.

Bare arms and legs flailed and she scrambled to her feet. She was wearing shorts and a T-shirt lettered STOWE SCHOOL across the chest. She was breathing hard.

The man continued to stand hands-on-hips, jut-jawed, and healthy enough to die of rosy cheeks. He was staring inquisitively at Nudger.

Claudia raked her fingers straight back through her tangled dark hair, moved to the stereo, and switched off the soft-porn rock number that was throbbing through the speakers.

Silence now. Heavy. Nudger experienced a falling sensation.

"We were doing aerobics," Claudia said. There was a bead of perspiration on the very tip of her nose. "This is Biff Archway. Biff, this is—"

"Aerobics?" Nudger interrupted.

"Sure," Archway said. "Aerobic exercises." He glanced over at Claudia's rapidly rising and falling chest. "Great for the heart and lungs."

Archway looked almost exactly as Nudger had imagined: medium height with a weight lifter's tapered body, clean-featured and aggressively handsome in the way of a college football hero grown to middle age and taking the best care of himself. Just a hell of a guy. Nudger noticed the living room had about it a musky smell of stale perspiration, like the bedroom after he and Claudia had made love.

"Claudia and I know each other from Stowe School," Archway said amiably.

Nudger nodded. "I know. You teach sex education out there. Isn't that the sort of thing that requires research?"

Archway looked again at Claudia, as if for some sort of signal to let him know how to treat this unwelcome intruder. Beyond him Nudger saw Claudia's clothes, including her panties and bra, laid out neatly on the sofa.

"Did the two of you change clothes in here?" he asked.

"I did," Claudia said. "Biff changed in the bedroom." She'd regained her composure and was giving Nudger her dark cautioning look. He was angering and embarrassing her. "Try to keep from making an ass of yourself," she told him.

"Too late for that," Nudger said. He knew that was true.

"Listen, sport," Archway said, stepping toward Nudger.

"Out!" Nudger said sharply, gripping him firmly by the arm. "Time for everyone named Biff to leave."

Archway didn't budge. Nudger was surprised by the hardness of the upper arm he was trying to clamp his fingers around.

"Don't!" Claudia warned. "Biff has a brown belt in karate, Nudger. Please, take it easy!"

Easy, hell! Nudger thought. He hunkered down and tried to push Archway toward the door. Archway shifted his weight subtly and Nudger stumbled a few feet beyond him, grasping empty air as he caught his balance. So the guy knew judo too, apparently.

"I suggest that you should be the one to leave," Archway said calmly.

Nudger charged him, swung with a looping right hand, found himself upside down in the air, then on his back on the floor.

All so sudden.

"Time for Nudger to leave," Archway said.

"Don't hurt him, Biff!" Claudia pleaded.

That got Nudger furious. He was on his feet again, moving in on Archway in a crouch. He shot out a straight left jab. Archway somehow grabbed his wrist, yanked, and Nudger found himself on the other side of the room.

"I'm finding it harder and harder not to hurt this jerk," Archway said. He assumed a distinctly Oriental fighting stance; even his features suddenly appeared Oriental.

Nudger went at him again. Archway shouted something that sounded like "Hii-yah!"

Nudger saw him shift his body sideways, then drop low and extend a hip. Archway had a hand beneath Nudger's arm, against his side, and Nudger was in the air, again about to land hard on his back. His injured rib seemed to catch fire and he drew in a breath that was almost a harsh scream. A lamp that must have been teetering on the edge of a table finally fell and dangled half on the floor by its stretched cord.

Something seemed to have snapped at the base of Nudger's spine this flight.

"Hey, you got some kind of bandage wrapped around you," Archway said, as if annoyed that he'd been tricked into not playing fair. "You better take it easy, sport."

Nudger got up slowly, a fist doubled behind him and pressed to the small of his back. He limped to the door, pain jolting through him with each step.

"Nudger!" Claudia called.

But Nudger was into the hall, on his way down the stairs. Archway was saying something he couldn't understand. Didn't want to hear, anyway.

Claudia again: "Damn you, Nudger, come back here!"

He could still hear her calling to him as he pushed through the vestibule door and lurched across the street to his car. Some of the neighbors stopped polishing and mowing to look.

He drove a few blocks down the street, then pulled to the curb. His side and back had almost stopped hurting. Now his hands were trembling; he was too upset to drive farther. He sat in the parked Volkswagen, glad that it was darker and people couldn't see the rage and humiliation that he knew were distorting his features.

This was one of the few times he wished he owned a gun. He knew that any other weapon against Archway would probably be useless, or turned against him. But a gun, death from ten feet away with the twitch of a finger on the trigger, almost as impersonal as fate, that was different. So very different. Thunder and deadly destiny. Archway could do nothing against that.

Nudger imagined the two of them, Archway and Claudia, turning their heads, surprised to see him again as he burst into the apartment. He could see their startled expressions, the fear in Archway's wide eyes when he saw the gun in Nudger's hand. Maybe he'd beg. Crawl. Maybe the bastard—

Nudger shook himself. "Jesus! . . ." he whispered harshly. What was he thinking? What was he considering?

And he was glad he didn't own a gun. He might have killed Archway.

He actually might have.

He wiped his hand over his perspiring face. There was no real difference between him and Curtis Colt, he realized. No difference.

A teenage boy and girl strolled past on the sidewalk, walking with difficulty because their arms were around each other, and stared at Nudger.

He felt sick. He started the engine and drove home.

25

When he got back to his apartment, Nudger stretched out on the sofa with the light out and worked at feeling sorry for himself.

It was even less difficult than he'd anticipated. Things had been piling up lately, bearing down on him. He thought about calling Candy Ann at the Ramada Inn, but Siberling might be there. A phone call was a bad idea, anyway, he decided. He knew he was in no condition to cheer up anyone. Right now, he was probably the last person who should talk to Candy Ann.

He lay thinking of how he might have handled Archway if only he'd thought to tackle the man and drag him down, wrestle with him, maybe even put some of those TV wrestling holds on him, the Bavarian Claw, or the Neutron Spinal Twist, not give him a chance to do his dancing act where the finale was Nudger soaring through the air. But he knew, really, that the younger and more powerful Archway would probably have subdued him in a wrestling match easily, and maybe even more painfully. The wholesome bastard probably ran ten miles a day. Probably lifted weights. Probably ate weights. Claudia could really pick them.

Claudia . . . He veered his mind away from Claudia, away from
that kind of agony. He tried to think about Curtis Colt, a man with
troubles that made Nudger's seem trivial. But that wasn't much
help. He, Nudger, was Nudger, and Colt was Colt and so not of as
much concern. Suffering was a solitary exercise. That was how
wars and executions worked.

Around midnight, Nudger's side and back stopped throbbing.
He rolled onto his left side, managed to work his body into a
reasonably comfortable position, and finally fell asleep.

In the morning, he limped into the bathroom and showered. The
steam and the stinging hot water relieved him of some of his stiff-
ness. Gradually increasing the temperature of the water, he stayed
in the stifling shower stall until he could barely breathe and had to
get out. The outer bathroom, which was probably over ninety degrees, felt refreshingly cool in contrast as Nudger stepped over the
edge of the tub.

He toweled dry slowly, and was walking okay by the time he'd
finished dressing.

It was eight-thirty, half an hour away from Curtis Colt's execution. Nudger got Mr. Coffee going, then went into the living room
and called Candy Ann at the Ramada Inn. He thought about what
Harold Benedict had said about the apartment phone possibly
being tapped, but he didn't give a damn. Not at the moment.

Siberling answered the phone in Room 220. Nudger couldn't
help wondering if the Napoleonic little lawyer had spent the night
there, found himself a Josephine. He mentally kicked himself for
thinking that way, blaming it on his painful experience of last
night at Claudia's.

"Where's Candy Ann?" he asked.

"She's working at the Right Steer," Siberling said. "The media
aren't covering the place now, or her trailer. They figure she's in
hiding, and they know the story, as far as she's concerned, is

going to end very soon. There'll be plenty of time to aggravate her later for in-depth interviews, if anybody's still interested.''

"Is the story going to end?" Nudger asked.

"Scalla has half an hour to change his mind," Siberling said, "but he isn't going to. He's an eye-for-an-eye kind of fella. Curtis is as good as gone.''

"Did you tell Candy Ann that?"

"No, I advised her to treat today as she would any other, to have faith that it was just another stage in the climb to Curtis Colt's eventual retrial. She's better off thinking that way and working, keeping busy, instead of sitting around suffering like Curtis.''

"She'll learn about his death while she's waiting tables,'' Nudger said. The mundaneness of that bothered him. Sweet rolls, cream for the coffee, and Death.

"She'll learn," Siberling said, "then she'll probably take a cab home and weep. She'll get over it, Nudger. She's young, and stronger than you think. She'll recover, and we did everything we could. Life will keep dealing people shitty cards, the world will keep turning. Case closed. Or it will be in . . . twenty-five minutes now.''

Siberling had finally lost interest and enthusiasm. Already he was thinking about his next case on his road to wherever his career might take him. Maybe he was being hard, maybe just sensible. Nudger wished he could be like that.

After hanging up on Siberling, he walked around the apartment, staring out the windows at nothing. It occurred to him that he'd never washed the outside storm windows. No one had. Whose responsibility were they? What was in the lease about that? He'd never thought about it before, and he wondered why it was worrying him now. He went into the kitchen and poured a cup of coffee. Might as well get really jittery.

He tried to take Siberling's advice to Candy Ann and treat this like any other morning.

Not looking at the clock, he began preparing breakfast.

He heated the frying pan, sprayed it with Pam, and broke two eggs into it. Then he slid two pieces of bread in the toaster and pushed down on the handle.

Orange juice. He told himself he wanted some orange juice.

On the way to the refrigerator, he switched on the radio on the counter. It was tuned to one of those twenty-four-hour all-talk stations. He tried not to think about what they'd soon have to talk about. Right now an astrologer was explaining how the stars could affect our ability to make love.

Nudger poured a glass of juice and returned to stand over the sizzling eggs. He noticed he'd broken one of the yolks and it had run in a pattern that resembled the state of Missouri. What the hell could that mean? Was it some kind of omen? Maybe he ought to call the astrologer at the station and find out about this. But then that wasn't her specialty; she read stars, not eggs.

He stood slouching in front of the stove and worried the eggs with a wood-handled spatula. The morning had started badly and wasn't getting better.

At ten minutes after nine, a newscaster somberly announced that Curtis Colt had been put to death in the electric chair. It had taken three minutes and several surges of electricity to kill him. He'd offered no last words before two thousand volts had turned him from something into nothing.

Immediately after the announcement, a Jefferson City interview with Governor Scalla was played. The governor assured the voters that the electric chair could be made to do its work faster and more humanely, and that now that this unpleasant but necessary task had been done, potential murderers would realize the seriousness of what they might be considering and society could sleep easier in its collective bed. Justice had been served, Scalla said. Only by taking life could we emphasize the value of life.

Nudger switched off the radio.

He went ahead and ate his eggs, but he skipped the toast.

26

Siberling was wrong. Candy Ann was in no condition to take a taxi home from the Right Steer. She had fainted when told of Curtis Colt's execution, and when she'd been revived, through her stammering and weeping she'd given the restaurant manager Nudger's number to call.

The aging White Knight to the rescue. By ten o'clock, Nudger had parked the VW in front of the Right Steer and was on his way inside to get Candy Ann.

The manager met Nudger just inside the door. He was wearing pointy-toed boots, jeans, and a fringed vinyl vest today. Everything but spurs and six-guns. He said his name was Mathewson and led Nudger through the dining area, then behind where the steaks were being broiled on an open grill, to a small office next to the kitchen.

Candy Ann was lying on a brown vinyl sofa that matched exactly the color of Mathewson's vest, as if material had been left over and put to practical use. She was calm now, but she'd been crying hard. Her eyes were reddened and swollen almost closed. They were the kind of eyes that made your own water when you looked at them.

When she saw Nudger, she reached inside herself for a smile. She found a faint one that would have to do. "Mr. Nudger . . ."

Mathewson said, "You can take her out the side door." He sounded impatient, worn down by Candy Ann and her trauma. This was a place of business, for chrissakes! The lunch crowd was already on his mental horizon; he could see their dust as they stam-

154

peded toward the swinging doors, hell-bent for the Buckeroo Special. "Take as long off as you need, Candy Ann," he added. "Your job will be here for you." Well, not such a bad guy after all.

Nudger thanked Mathewson for calling him, then led Candy Ann by the arm into the hot parking lot. Asphalt stuck to their soles. The sun was like a velvet weight pressing down.

"You want to go home?" he asked.

She nodded, then kept her head bowed. She'd never looked so frail; she seemed to have lost twenty pounds overnight.

Nudger held the car door open for her; she was, especially now, the kind of woman who aroused male protective impulses and was naturally treated as a lady.

He walked around and got in behind the wheel, then edged the Volkswagen out onto Watson Road and drove toward Placid Grove Trailer Park.

This threatened to be the hottest day of the summer, and the inside of the trailer was stifling. As soon as they'd entered, Nudger switched on the air conditioner.

Candy Ann slumped in the small chair in the living room and used her palms to wipe perspiration from her face. The sweat stung her eyes, and that got her crying again. She didn't seem able to stop. It was the kind of deep, racking sobbing that perpetuated itself, that could lead to complete physical and mental exhaustion.

"Do you have a regular doctor?" Nudger asked.

She shook her head. "Never needed one much. I've been down to People's Medical Clinic a few times, for female things. They assigned me to a Dr. Ochebow, a foreigner."

Nudger phoned the clinic, talked to Dr. Ochebow, and explained the situation. Ochebow had a high voice and what sounded like an Indian accent. He was difficult to understand, but he seemed sympathetic and competent. He said he'd phone in a prescription for a sedative.

"Which of the neighbors do you get along with best?" Nudger asked, after he'd hung up.

Candy Ann thought about that. "Wanda Scathers, in the trailer behind this one." She stopped talking for a moment to ride out a sobbing jag. "The one with the brown awnings."

Nudger told Candy Ann he'd be back soon, then went outside and stepped over a twisted wire fence between the two trailers. A small grayish dog scrambled out from under the Scathers' trailer and started yapping at him as if it had never laid eyes on anything quite so contemptible and threatening. He noticed that its ears were laid back flat against its head, so it was scared and probably bluffing. Or so he told himself as he advanced and the dog retreated, matching him precisely step for step, as if they were performing an intricate Latin dance maneuver Nudger vaguely remembered from the movies.

"Stop it, Buffy! Right now!" the woman in the trailer's open back door shouted.

Magic voice, magic words. Buffy abruptly calmed down. He turned up his pinkish nose at Nudger, blinked several times, then retreated back beneath the trailer where it was cooler, as if to say all this wasn't worth his trouble anyway. Dogs could be fickle that way, not unlike people.

Nudger walked over to the woman, who had waddled down the metal steps and was standing in the shade of the back-door awning. She was in her forties, and hadn't been pretty even twenty years and fifty pounds ago. Her hair was thin and scraggly, and she was wearing bright pink slacks and a clashing green blouse with dark stains down the front. In her right hand was a paint-smeared screwdriver long and thick enough to use as a crowbar.

She looked at Nudger, then glanced down for a second at the screwdriver in her hand. "Been fixin' things," she explained, not smiling.

Nudger tried a smile and introduced himself. "You're a friend of Candy Ann Adams, aren't you?"

She nodded. "We know each other. Talked over the fence from time to time." ·

"She's suffered a shock," Nudger said. "A friend of hers was killed and she's pretty upset."

Wanda appeared surprised. Apparently she didn't read the newspapers or watch what passed for news on TV. She hadn't known about Curtis' execution and his relationship with Candy Ann. And, obviously, Candy Ann hadn't considered her enough of a friend to confide in.

"Was this person killed in some kinda accident?" she asked.

"You could say that. And you could help Candy Ann by driving over to Walgreen's Drugstore on Watson and picking up a prescription her doctor phoned in."

"How come you ain't going?"

"I think I need to stay with her, the way she is."

Wanda still wasn't sure about Nudger, the ominous stranger. What might he be up to? She peered around him, down along the side of Candy Ann's trailer. "Can't tell, the past several months, whether she's home or not," she said.

"She's home," Nudger said. "And I'm worried about her and telling you the truth. You want to phone her to check?"

But the offer itself was enough. "I guess not." She contorted an arm to reach behind her and scratch between her shoulder blades with the screwdriver. "I'd like to help. Who knows, I might need the same sorta help myself someday. What kinda prescription?"

"Just a sedative to help her sleep off some of her grief. Nothing strong." He looked into Wanda's small brown eyes, imagining her thoughts. Prescription medicine. Drugs. He couldn't blame her for being skeptical. "Everything's legal," he said. "I promise. Nothing crossed but my heart."

"I didn't mean to act like I didn't trust you."

"That's okay," Nudger said. "You should be careful."

"That's the truth, way people are these days."

A thin girl about ten, with Wanda's tiny, vacuous eyes, came to the door. She stood with one hand lightly touching the doorjamb, as if to maintain contact with reality.

Wanda noticed her. "Can you watch your baby sister for a while, Lou Jane? I gotta run an errand."

The girl nodded silently.

Wanda turned back to Nudger, waiting. A large fly touched down on her shoulder. She absently brushed it away and it buzzed into the trailer.

Nudger gave her a ten-dollar bill. "The prescription's in Candy Ann's name, phoned in by Dr. Ochebow from the People's Clinic."

Wanda nodded, pocketed the money, then tossed the screwdriver past Lou Jane onto the trailer floor. Nudger heard it bounce and then roll into the dimness behind the child.

"Back as soon as I can, Lou Jane," Wanda said. "You keep your hands outa them potato chips." She walked heavily around toward the front of the trailer.

Nudger heard a car start after three long, grinding attempts, then saw her drive down Tranquillity Lane in a dented blue Datsun.

He looked at Lou Jane and smiled. Deadpan, she quietly closed the door on him. Such a way he had with women.

He climbed back over the wire fence, knocking it flat and then stooping to bend it erect again. Buffy took that as a signal for mild aggression and emitted a few halfhearted growls from the shadows beneath the trailer. But it was a hot, hot day, and one burst of ferociousness by one small dog was enough.

The pills took effect less than an hour after Candy Ann had swallowed the first one. She wanted to sleep where she was sitting in the living room chair, but Nudger forced her to stand and helped her into the tiny bedroom. He was surprised to see that most of the room was taken up by a water bed. He guided her down onto the bed, then timed his actions with the waves so he could remove her sensible waitress shoes.

"Lightnin'," she muttered. "Hit the old tree behind the house. Left it all black and charred. Lordy! Don't let it get me, hear? *Hear*?"

"I hear," Nudger said. He patted her forehead and waited for her to be quiet, to sleep.

When she was breathing evenly, he left her alone.

He didn't think he should leave the trailer. He had nowhere important to go, anyway. He sat on the sofa in the living room and read dog-eared back issues of *People* magazine while Candy Ann slept.

After learning a lot about Johnny Carson's diet, Debra Winger's taste in men, Walter Cronkite's boat, and a history of show-business deals struck in hot tubs, Nudger fell asleep himself.

Biff Archway was stripped to the waist, dressed like a pirate and struggling with the spoked wheel. Debra Winger was lounging on the deck in a bikini, pointing languidly toward land. Nudger was being interviewed for *People* by Walter Cronkite on Cronkite's boat.

"So they executed him," Nudger was saying. "Zap! Just like that. Well, not just like that. It took a little longer than they expected. In fact, a lot longer. His flesh sizzled like bacon."

Johnny Carson peered down from the bridge and grinned. "How dead *is* he?" he asked.

Cronkite laughed like an amiable grandfather. Archway winked at Debra Winger, who smiled. Lightning danced on the horizon.

"Thar she blows!" Archway yelled lustily. He waved his cutlass.

A woman's voice, not Debra Winger's, said, "Mr. Nudger?"

The trailer was dim. Candy Ann was standing over Nudger. Or was he dreaming?

"Why does that bastard get to steer the boat?" he asked.

"Mr. Nudger, wake up." She was shaking his shoulder.

His body jerked and he sat up on the sofa. He looked around, remembering. The boat was gone. So was the ocean.

"You okay?" he asked.

"Better," Candy Ann said. "You been dreaming?"

"I sure hope so." Nudger wiped at his eyes and ran his tongue around the inside of his mouth. His brain was still fogged from sleep. His side was aching from his uncomfortable position on the sofa. "What time is it?"

"Almost nine-thirty," she said. "We both slept for a long spell."

"I'm still tired," Nudger mumbled, and struggled to his feet. A dull pain crept up his right side, reached his armpit, then retreated halfway. It leveled off and was bearable.

"Will you stay?" Candy Ann asked. "Please!"

"Stay?"

"I need someone with me tonight. All night." She'd moved closer and he smelled gin on her breath.

"You've been drinking."

"Not much."

"You can't mix booze with those pills. Dangerous."

"I ain't had another pill." She was walking now, into the bedroom, glancing back at him.

Nudger followed.

He stood next to her by the bed, thinking about Curtis Colt, not yet buried. He was repulsed by what he wanted so desperately to do. Life as opposed to death.

Candy Ann knew what was in his mind, sensed his desire and his revulsion.

"Not sex," she said hastily. "I need someone to hold me, is all. Tonight I'm alone more than I ever been."

Her words released him. He nodded and lay down with her on the water bed, feeling the mattress undulate as she moved up against him, scooting on her elbows and knees.

She sighed, as if for the first time in hours she was finally relaxing. He held her tightly and she dug her chin sharply into his chest. Then a sudden looseness ran through her body as tension at last flowed from her.

Her immense weariness was contagious. Nudger realized he probably couldn't climb out of the comfortable bed even if he mustered all his willpower. He wasn't sure if that was because he was still tired from mental strain, or from not enough or too much sleep, or if he wanted to stay there as long as possible and clutch the fragile, bony form of Candy Ann to him. It was as if he could absorb her pain, and she his.

She seemed to drift into sleep again almost immediately.

It was past midnight before Nudger slept again, but he was content lying quietly awake until then.

27

Nudger left Candy Ann asleep the next morning, making his way out of the trailer silently and driving home over empty early-Sunday streets. He'd realized what might happen if he stayed with her that day. And there was something else, something nibbling at the edges of his consciousness. It was more than the fact that her blind optimism had affected him, made him believe in life over death despite pronouncements of doom by the state and by Curtis Colt's own lawyer, and then left him saddened and disappointed. There was a frayed loose end somewhere, occasionally tickling the back of Nudger's neck.

After showering and changing clothes at his apartment, he read the account of Colt's execution in the morning *Post-Dispatch*. Colt reportedly had rejected the presence of a clergyman and had walked calmly to the execution chamber. He had been quiet and composed until just before the switch was to be thrown, then he'd panicked and struggled. But only for an instant. The high voltage had grabbed him, distorted his struggles into grotesque contortions. Three powerful surges. Flesh had burned, sparks had flown, smoke had risen. Witnesses had turned away. The *Post* had an editorial about the execution on the op-ed page. They hadn't liked it, didn't want it to happen again. Good for them. Too late for Curtis Colt, who had gone to meet his Maker fortified with a last meal of White Castle hamburgers and Pepsi.

Nudger turned to the sports page and found that the winning streak had also expired: the Cardinals had finally lost a ball game. "Braves Bury Cards 10–0," the headline read. There was no joy anywhere in the paper today.

At eleven o'clock, Nudger phoned Candy Ann. She'd been awake about an hour, she said, and wondered where he was. She didn't ask him why he'd left. She knew why. Her voice was thick from too much sleep and too much grief, but she seemed composed now and resigned to the fact that Curtis was gone. She was young, Siberling had said. Stronger than Nudger thought. She'd recover. Maybe Siberling knew about such things. Nudger hoped so.

"Send me your bill, Mr. Nudger," she said, all business again. "I'll pay it somehow. Maybe not right away, but someday. I promise you that."

Nudger thought about the cramped trailer and her near-minimum-wage job at the Right Steer. Then he thought about her hill-country pride. "I'll mail it," he said. "But there won't be a due date on it. I won't worry about it and I don't want you to."

She was silent for a while before speaking. "I do thank you, Mr. Nudger." There was a weary finality in the way she said it. She'd gone up against the world for love and lost, and was settling into resignation.

Nudger told her to call him if she needed any more help of any kind, then hung up. An emotion he couldn't identify was lodged in his throat. He swallowed. That helped, but not much.

He sat for a long time staring at the phone.

It might be a good idea to call Harold Benedict tomorrow morning, he thought, find out if there was any work available. Life went on. So did expenses. Eileen would be calling. That was a sure bet. So would Union Electric and his landlord and the phone company. Everyone could form a line.

Nudger decided not to worry about that. Benedict would have something. And Nudger was still due to be paid for the Calvin Smith photographs. Anyway, it might be weeks before a steady diet of Danny's coffee and doughnuts could prove fatal. There was enough of that most precious commodity in this world, time. What the old woman in the liquor store and what Curtis Colt had run out of. Time. What whittled away at flesh and empires. What hurt and healed and always won its dark victory.

What Nudger had too much of today.

Monday morning a copy of the latest *St. Louis Voyeur* was stuffed into Nudger's mailbox in the vestibule of his apartment building. He wasn't a subscriber, so with a certain dread he withdrew the thin weekly newspaper from the tarnished brass box and unfolded it.

Though he was somewhat prepared, it was still a shock. The *Voyeur* hadn't given up on Candy Ann, hadn't the decency to allow her some breathing space. There was a front-page photo layout of the entire Curtis Colt affair, including shots of Colt being arrested, a long view of Olson's Liquor Emporium, Colt being led to his execution, and a candid close-up of an apparently sobbing Candy Ann above the caption "Wages of Lover's Sin."

The last photograph, "Solace After Heartbreak," was of Nudger stealthily stepping outside into the brightening morning and closing Candy Ann's trailer door behind him. His face was turned three-quarters toward the camera, his features highlighted by the rising sun. The shot was a little fuzzy because of the long lens the photographer had used, but there was no doubt as to the identity of the man in the photo. There was what appeared to be an expression of guilt on his face, though Nudger knew it was really the result of him squinting in the sudden morning light.

He felt embarrassed, then angry. Then he told himself nobody read the rag of a paper anyway.

But he knew better. People in his line of work read the *Voyeur*. So did some of the people who might hire him. Even people who couldn't read bought the *Voyeur*. The photograph would be misunderstood and bad for business.

But then, business was plenty bad already.

The hell with it. Nudger carried the paper upstairs, wadded it tightly, and dropped it into the wastebasket in the cabinet beneath the kitchen sink. It made a solid, satisfying sound hitting the rest of the trash.

Then he stood for a moment, rubbing the back of his neck and turning in a slow circle. The sun was brilliant on the window over the sink, casting a weblike shadow of the glass's corner crack onto the bright counter. A large wasp, reveling in the morning heat, buzzed exploringly against the pane from frame to frame, found no opening, then zigzagged away. Nudger stopped turning and stood still and watched it, until the mere speck that it had become blended with the leaves of a tree and could no longer be discerned. He wondered how long the wasp would live if it didn't fall victim to a bird or exterminator. It struck him as tragic that any creature should miss the opportunity to live out its allotted time. Cruel nature, crueler mankind.

He knew he couldn't stay away. He'd known it since yesterday.

Before he had breakfast, before he called Harold Benedict or left to look at his office mail or checked his answering machine, he put on his blue sport coat and a dark tie and drove to Curtis Colt's funeral.

28

It was a state-funded affair, with only a graveside ceremony at a paupers' cemetery in south St. Louis. Nudger had noticed the date and time of burial while reading newspaper accounts of Colt's execution, and they had lodged, cold and nagging, in his mind.

There were about a dozen people gathered around the grave, including the state-appointed clergyman. Most of them were pallbearers, also paid by the state. Lester was there, looking more bereaved then anyone, wearing an oversized winter-wool sport jacket over a T-shirt. There was an older couple who appeared bored with the ceremony. Welborne Colt hadn't attended. He and his brother had reached the final parting still separated by antagonism and distance.

Candy Ann was standing about a hundred feet away from the clergyman, off to the side of the gleaming wood casket. Her straw-colored hair glowed with the morning. In the wash of bright sunlight, she looked like a child playing dress-up in black.

When she saw Nudger, she averted her eyes. He was sure she'd gotten her complimentary copy of the *Voyeur*, as he had. A great thing to wake up to on the day of your fiancé's funeral.

The preacher, who himself resembled a cadaver and was of indeterminate religion, adjusted his dark suit on his thin frame and made a vague crosslike motion with his right hand. Nudger noticed several people, including a man with a tripod-mounted camera, stationed on the grave-strewn hill above Curtis' coffin. The media would stop only after Colt was buried, and maybe not even then. Certain crimes, and their aftermaths, caught and held the public's attention. Nudger knew a telephoto lens was probably trained in close-up on Candy Ann now as the photographer, possibly from the *Voyeur*, hoped for an expression of grief, a tear. If he really got lucky, she'd faint.

The clergyman rambled on about life and death, gesticulating grandly, playing for the press. Where Nudger was standing, the man's voice came across merely as a monotonous drone. Everyone around the grave was shifting their weight from leg to leg, perspiring heavily, wishing the clergyman would finish sending Colt on his way. Only Candy Ann stood perfectly still, though, like Nudger, she was probably too far away to understand what the preacher was saying.

A blue jay in a nearby pin oak began chattering angrily, noisily, upstaging the preacher, who turned briefly and glared at it. The jay cocked its head to the side, as if to get a better angle of vision, and stared back insolently with a bright eye, a look it probably usually reserved for worms. The clergyman made up his mind to ignore the winged interloper. The jay hopped down onto a lower branch, among sunlit leaves, and really started raising hell. That seemed to hurry the gaunt man of the cloth along.

Finally the service was over. The jay stopped its clacking as if in relief. Candy Ann walked to the single floral spray by the grave, plucked a blossom, and laid it gently on the lid of the casket. The clergyman rested a bony hand on her shoulder, but she ignored him. He was part of Curtis' imposed untimely death and could in no way comfort her.

After standing motionless for a few minutes, she turned and walked away. Nudger saw the photographer with the tripod and long lens straighten up from his camera and say something to the man next to him. Everyone began drifting toward the parked cars.

Something tugged at Nudger's arm. He turned to see Lester Colt beside him, red-eyed and stricken-looking. His face was puffier than usual, and he reeked of cheap, perfumy cologne or shaving lotion mingled with perspiration.

"I figure you did your best, Mr. Nudger," he said. He sniffled. "Want you to know there ain't no hard feelings 'cause you couldn't save Curtis."

Nudger nodded, feeling uncomfortable. "We did what we could," he said. "I'm sorry, Lester." Over Lester's shoulder he saw Candy Ann get into a waiting County cab, a flash of pale leg against the black of her dress.

"Welborne shoulda been here, don't you think?"

"I think so," Nudger said. He didn't feel like giving Welborne a break. "It was the least he could have done. His own brother." Nudger meant it.

The taxi carrying Candy Ann wound along the cemetery's narrow gravel road, flashing through patches of deep shade. It paused at tall black iron gates hinged open on stone pillars, then turned out into the traffic. Nudger could see Candy Ann's wide black hat through the cab's rear window. She didn't look back.

"She did okay by Curtis after all," Lester said, watching with Nudger as the cab disappeared beyond the trees. He smiled, looked over at the grave, and sniffled again.

"How did you get here?" Nudger asked. There were no more parked cars now other than his VW and a van belonging to one of the media people.

"Took a bus. Couple of buses. My car's broke down."

"Where you going now?"

"Back to work. I got to. The foreman said I could have the rest of the day free, but I'll be better off taking it out on the freight, what I feel. Work's kinda like medicine, don't you think?"

"Like medicine," Nudger agreed. He'd often fled into the diversion of hard work himself. But he knew that eventually work wasn't enough; at a certain point people had to turn and face whatever they were running from or holding at bay.

He told Lester he was going his way and would drop him off at Commerce Freightlines. Two bearded men in work clothes were hanging around the grave, in the shade of a small canvas awning

that had been set up, waiting for the last of the mourners to leave
so they could lower the casket.

He started the VW and followed the path of the taxi along the
winding gravel road.

At the tall gates, he remembered something Wanda Scathers had
said, and he knew what had been bothering him since the day of
Curtis Colt's death.

He twisted the vent window to direct fresh air into the car, to
combat Lester's smarmy cologne, and accelerated out into heavy
traffic that ran parallel to the cemetery's black iron fence.

Beside him, Lester was talking incessantly, but Nudger wasn't
listening.

29

Benedict would have work to be farmed out soon, he assured
him, when Nudger phoned him. The proprietor of Enchanted Night
Escort Service had hired Benedict and Schill to defend the service
in a suit brought by a former employee who'd been fired for pros-
tituting herself.

Nudger decided that the morning was following its established
gloomy course. Everything in the office was sticky with humidity.

"The escort service is really on the up and up," Benedict explained. "It provides women to accompany out-of-town executives
to social functions. The fees are high and the employees have
strict, written rules of behavior; they're escorts, and escorts only."

That ran contrary to Nudger's concept of an escort service, but
he said nothing. His middle-class background might be showing.

"One of the escorts, a Sandra McClain, went beyond the call of duty one night with an undercover cop, was arrested, and claimed she was a housewife working part-time and had been coerced by the escort service into prostitution. The only way she could continue working, she said, to provide food for the children; yeah, she really said that. So she and her out-of-work husband filed suit, probably hoping to save face more than anything else.''

Nudger wondered if the woman might be telling the truth, caught in a trap that was perhaps so disturbingly commonplace that it had taken on the exaggeration of burlesque and people refused to take it seriously.

"How do I figure into this?" he asked.

"Ms. McClain was a prostitute before she worked for the escort service, spread her wares all over town. She might still be lying down for fun and profit even as the court date nears. We need you to establish beyond doubt that she'd been in the sporting life before. Or better yet, that she still is.''

That didn't sound too difficult. If the McClain woman had been a high-priced prostitute, he knew the people who would know about it. Unless she was a free-lancer. Then he'd have to dig deeper, follow her.

"Sandra McClain is out of the city now," Benedict said. "In the Bahamas. Where else would you expect to find a woman with hungry children at home? She'll be back in a week, tan and fiesty. That's when our client will decide whether he wants a detective on her. When he gives the official okay, you're on the case.''

It sounded kind of indefinite to Nudger, but he thanked Benedict.

"Tough about the Curtis Colt thing," Benedict said.

Nudger agreed, thinking that "tough" was a bit of an understatement.

"He suffered, according to the paper," Benedict said. "You'd think they'd have something like that perfected after all these years. But then, I guess executions aren't supposed to be fun.''

"Why not?" Nudger said. "Don't be a wet blanket.''

Benedict spoke in a careful manner indicating he was weighing words. Lawyer paranoia. The old phone-tap syndrome. "Colt can't be helped now, Nudger. I guess you're going to let that case drop."

"Yeah," Nudger lied. "Unless somebody hires me to try to raise the dead, it's over."

"I, uh, saw your photograph in the *Voyeur.* Yellow scandal journalism. You want me to call the rag, talk lawyer talk, throw a scare into them?"

"Thanks for the offer," Nudger said, "but you probably wouldn't scare them, only get them mad. Then they'd figure out an excuse to sue *me*. I'm afraid of litigation, putting my fate in the hands of twelve people I might be tearing away from the afternoon TV soaps."

"Objection sustained," Benedict said. "Take care of yourself, Nudger. Stay away from . . . trouble."

Trouble being Candy Ann Adams.

"I'll avoid it as if it were a downed power line," Nudger said, and hung up.

Early the next morning, he began watching Candy Ann's trailer.

At eight-thirty she emerged, dressed in her yellow waitress uniform, and got into another taxi. She moved slowly, as if mired in her grief. Her hair was combed differently, parted and flung to the side. It made her appear older.

Nudger followed in his battered Volkswagen as the cab drove her the four and a half miles to her job at the Right Steer. She didn't look around as she paid the driver and walked inside through the Old-West-saloon swinging doors. Nudger waited for the sounds of a tinkling piano, of whooping, of breaking glass, and gunshots. Then he remembered the place was full of Muzak and baked potatoes.

At six that evening, another cab drove her home, making a brief stop at a Kroger supermarket. She came out of the store carrying a single small paper sack, got back in the cab, and continued on her way.

It went that way for the next couple of days, trailer to work to trailer, all by taxi. A lonely ritual. Candy Ann had no visitors other than the plain brown paper bag she took home every night.

During the day, while she was safely at work, Nudger spent his time unobtrusively talking to her neighbors. He avoided Wanda Scathers, thinking she might tip Candy Ann that he was hanging around the trailer court.

Posing as an insurance investigator, it didn't take him long to learn what there was to know in a metal-and-wheeled neighborhood where people made it a point not to meddle in their neighbors' business, but were bored and glad to gossip nonetheless—if the right questions were asked in the right way. He got a fuller picture of Candy Ann and Curtis Colt, though not necessarily an accurate one.

Sometimes, sitting melting in the Volkswagen in the middle of one of the Sultry City's legendary summer heat waves, Nudger wondered if what he was doing was really worthwhile. Curtis Colt was, after all, dead, and had never been his client. Still, there were responsibilities that went beyond the job. Or maybe they were actually the essence of the job.

Thursday, after Candy Ann had left for work, Nudger used his honed Visa card to slip the flimsy lock on her trailer door, and let himself in.

He was alone now where Curtis Colt had spent so much time with Candy Ann, and time by himself. Nudger's heart began hammering and his stomach turned over a few times. He always felt like this when he was trespassing. An unhealthy respect for the law.

Though Candy Ann had switched off the air conditioner before leaving only minutes ago, the inside of the trailer was getting warm fast. It wasn't well insulated, and the sun was beating out a rising rhythm on the aluminum roof. Nudger didn't want to turn

the air conditioner back on and possibly draw the attention of
Wanda Scathers, who might know that Candy Ann had left for
work by this time of the morning.

Patiently, methodically, he began searching the trailer.

It took him over an hour to find what he was looking for. It had
been well hidden, in a cardboard box above a loose ceiling panel
in the bathroom. After examining the box's contents—almost
seven hundred dollars in loot from Curtis Colt's brief life of crime,
and another object Nudger wasn't surprised to see—he resealed
the box and replaced it above the panel.

Curtis Colt, you desperado, you, Nudger thought. Then he
thought about Tom, and he decided, heat or no heat, that he'd
continue following Candy Ann. He owed her, and Curtis, that
much.

He knew her work schedule, which made things much easier for
him. For now, she would be safe at work at the Right Steer and
didn't require his attention.

He made sure he left the trailer as he'd found it, then went back
outside where, for at least a few minutes, he felt cooler.

When Nudger got back to his office, Danny told him Claudia
had been by early that morning, looking for him. She'd had a
Dunker Delite and a carton of milk, waited around for a while,
then she'd given Danny a note to forward to Nudger.

The note was in blue pen, stroked in her neat teacher's hand-
writing. It said simply that she wanted to see Nudger late this
afternoon or tonight, and asked him to come by her apartment
anytime after four. She needed to talk about something important,
she said. It was signed "Love, Claudia."

Nudger didn't know quite how to feel about that. But then he
didn't have a choice about how he felt. Nobody did. That was
what caused so many knotty problems for so many people and kept
him in business.

There was another message from Eileen on Nudger's answering

machine. He listened to it only long enough to learn why she'd been trying to talk with him. He had indeed paid her only half of last month's alimony. Not only that, her lawyer had a file on the dates of all the late payments made by Nudger, and used some kind of sliding formula to calculate the interest Eileen claimed she was owed. The interest rate was several points higher than the prime rate, which Nudger always thought was really the rate banks charged their *worst* customers. But then there was little doubt that First National Eileen considered him to be her very worst customer.

Nudger knew he'd better pay Eileen the other half of the alimony soon. The demand for accumulated interest was probably a bluff, engineered to aggravate, and could be ignored. He wished she'd leave him alone. She had more money than he had. She could afford her pistol of a lawyer.

He folded Claudia's note and slid it into his shirt pocket. Life could be infinitely complicated. Mother hadn't told him there'd be years like this.

30

The apartment on Wilmington was neat and smelled of lemon-scented furniture wax, as if Claudia had just a moment ago finished cleaning and everything was still precisely in place. Maybe she wanted to talk to Nudger in surroundings as orderly as possible, so that their conversation would take on the same symmetry and manageability.

She was wearing her plain navy-blue dress and had her dark hair pulled back and pinned behind her ears, from where it was allowed to fall to below her shoulders. She looked startlingly beautiful to Nudger, her lean features made perfect by the late-afternoon light. It was four o'clock exactly. Nudger needed to see Claudia as early as possible in order to get to the Right Steer when Candy Ann got off work.

Candy Ann was on Claudia's mind, too. When Nudger had sat down on the sofa, she said, "Someone at the school was kind enough to show me your photograph in the paper. The one of you stepping down out of a trailer, wearing an expression that must have been a lot like Lancelot's when he left Guinevere's room." A crisp, almost reprimanding tone had crept into her voice.

"I don't think *Camelot* reads quite like that."

"I was striving for effect."

"This someone who showed you the photograph, was his name Archway?"

She shrugged with feigned nonchalance. "It doesn't matter." She was nervous. She took a few steps left, a few right, and wound up standing again in front of Nudger. "Since you spent the night with that girl, I thought maybe we could find some common ground, come to an understanding."

"You don't object that I saw her?"

"I don't have the right to object. Not to anyone you see. And vice versa. That's what I keep trying to get across to you."

"How do you know I spent the night with her?" Nudger asked. Claudia seemed slightly surprised. "The newspaper said so."

"Oh, I didn't know; I only looked at the photographs, then threw my copy away. I haven't believed anything in that paper since the crippled-UFO story. The one where aliens broke into a Shell station and stole an ordinary automobile battery—"

"Are you going to tell me you didn't sleep with her?" Claudia interrupted. Nudger thought he picked up a note of jealousy in the question. Yes, he was sure of it.

"I slept with her," he said. He watched Claudia wince ever so slightly. "But without sex. Her fiancé was ritualistically toasted to death that day; she needed somebody with her. That was what all our time together was about. She needed consoling.''

"And you happened to be the one to console her. All night."

"That's how it went," Nudger said.

Claudia sat down in the chair near the window. The filtered light streaming through the sheer curtains made her look ten years younger, softened her features yet lent them the intensity of youth. He recognized the bloodless, pale tightness at the corners of her lips, the subtle flare of her nostrils. She was feeling plenty ornery now, mad that she was put in the position of having made love to Archway while here was Nudger saying he'd been chaste since their argument, a saint of a guy. This was embarrassing and infuriating.

"I've always heard that men's consciences didn't apply below the belt line," she said.

"That's true about us only up to around age forty."

"It isn't important. The thing is, you spent the night with that woman. I confess I suffered some of the jealousy you must have felt when you found me with Biff. Some of the pain."

"Jesus, Claudia, a guy named Biff."

Her dark eyes narrowed. "Are you making a joke of this?"

"No."

"I want us to start seeing each other again, under different circumstances. I want to see other men occasionally, and you can see other women."

"By 'other men,' do you mean Archway?"

She shook her head. "No. He doesn't really matter. Never did. Besides, he's dating the girls' field-hockey coach, and has been for the past several months."

"She might be more his type. Does she crush the can after she drinks her beer?"

"Ease up, Nudger." A warning, not issued lightly.

"If Biff is out of the picture, and you want me back in, why do you have to go out with other men? Are you suddenly becoming nymphomaniacal?"

Her voice rose; she was strung even tighter than Nudger had thought. "Sex has nothing, or at least not everything, to do with it. Dr. Oliver told me you'd been to see him, that he'd explained things to you. Can't you understand and accept this independence and freedom in our relationship?"

"It will take some getting used to," Nudger said. He got up, walked into the kitchen, and got a can of beer from the refrigerator, making himself at home. Miller Lite was in there, not his brand. Whose, then? Biff's and the hockey coach's? He returned to the living room, wiping foam from his chin. "I'm not sure I can get used to it."

"I don't want to hurt you," Claudia said. "That's the thing I've never wanted in all of this. But the marriage with Ralph, what happened to end it . . . I need to break out of the box that put me in. Completely out. I need to discover who I really am."

That kind of talk made Nudger mad. "That's college-sophomore rhetoric, Claudia. What next? Are you going to tie a bandana around your head and hitchhike cross-country? It's the wrong decade for that. The people who did that kind of thing are living in condos and driving Volvos now, or playing Vegas. If you want to find out who you really are, check your driver's license."

She stood up, her fists clenched. Uh-oh! He knew he'd gone too far. Maybe way too far.

"Damn it, Nudger! If you don't care about me, the hell with you! That's how trapped I am in myself; the only way I can try to express it is in clichés and stilted sixties dialogue. If I could understand and articulate it, do you think I'd be suffering from it?"

"Probably not, according to Oliver," Nudger said.

"Don't criticize Dr. Oliver. He saved my life."

Which was more or less true.

She was calmer now. She didn't want to admit that Nudger had also saved her life, but she realized it and it sobered her. Right now, he didn't want her gratitude.

He took a swig of beer, walked over, and kissed her on the

mouth. That felt good. Throw a little unexpected machismo on her, like in the movies. Gets 'em every time.

"What the hell's wrong with you?" she asked, and shoved him away so hard he almost tumbled backward. "I'm trying to talk."

"Maybe all this talk is what's wrong between us." Well, that and timing.

"Fuck you, Nudger. If that's the way you're thinking, go back to your scrawny blonde."

"Ah, you're more jealous than you thought! Dr. Oliver would say that was good for you."

"You son of a bitch!" She picked up a magazine from a table and threw it at him so hard it separated in midair, pages fluttering all over the room. She was left clutching the ripped and crumpled cover in her fist.

He wondered what was going on. Never had he seen her lose her temper this way. He liked it. Archway might flip him around like pizza crust, but he could handle this one. Could he ever!

He dived in on her low, grabbed her around the waist, and wrestled her to the carpet. She was strong, but he'd surprised her. That felt good.

She pounded his back with her fists. "Rape!" she said. "This is goddamned rape!"

"Robbery," Nudger told her, rolling on top of her. "I only want your purse."

"You know I don't have a purse!" she shouted, as he bit her earlobe. "Ouch, you idiot! Why did you do that?"

"I don't know," Nudger said, "maybe it is rape. I suppose I have options."

"The neighbors!" she said. "The neighbors around here will hear this and get up a petition to have me move. You don't know these people!"

"You're probably their entertainment," he said. "They have genitalia; they understand."

"Nudger, I'm serious!"

He ran a fingertip lightly along the side of her neck until she twitched involuntarily. She grabbed a handful of his hair and yanked hard, twisting.

"That feel sexy?" she asked.

"Makes me wish I wore a toupee. The joke'd be on you."

"Some rapist."

She released her grip and let her hand drop. There was a strand of hair snagged beneath one of her fingernails.

Nudger was out of breath. Middle-aged guy rolling around on the carpet. Whew! Out of shape. Not Biff.

She shoved him off her and he fell to the side, laughing. They were both laughing, but Claudia was holding her ear, not laughing as hard as he was.

She sat cross-legged next to him. After a while, she bent down and kissed him gently on the forehead.

"Stay with me tonight," she said.

"Under our new agreement?"

She nodded, smiling down at him.

He rolled over onto his hands and knees, caught his breath, and managed to get to his feet. His side was aching but he didn't care.

"Can't stay," he said. "Not tonight."

She stood up gracefully and brushed the wrinkles out of her dress. She wanted to ask him where he was going, but she wouldn't.

"I'll try to come back later. That is, if you aren't going to be with Archway. I've still got my key; it's just been stabbing me in the hip."

"I told you, I don't plan to see Biff again. What about you? Do you plan on seeing Candy Ann Adams anymore?"

Nudger nodded, tucking in his shirt. "I'm going to see her tonight," he said. "Business."

Claudia didn't comment on that, but it was obvious that she disapproved. She pulled a bobby pin from the side of her hair and clamped it in her teeth, rearranged a few errant strands, then replaced it. All very quickly and smoothly. Elegantly. The deftness of women with bobby pins always amazed him.

He said, "Mostly business, anyway."

He went out in a hurry and closed the door behind him, leaving Claudia alone to get used to their new arrangement.

As he was walking toward the stairs, he thought he heard something break inside the apartment, but he wasn't sure.

The neighbors remembered him from last time. The ones who'd been mowing then were polishing now, the ones who'd been polishing were mowing. They stopped working for a moment to stare. The last time they'd seen him he was walking doubled over like a guy who'd just been shot everywhere that wasn't fatal. He wondered how much they knew about him and Claudia. And about Claudia and Biff Archway. He stared back and they resumed their tidy tasks with fresh diligence.

Nudger started the Volkswagen and pulled away from the curb to the racketing of a dozen power mowers, on his way to the Right Steer Steakhouse.

Halfway down the block, an ancient, gray-haired guy buffing a vintage station wagon grinned wolfishly and gave him a jaunty salute.

31

Nudger waited in the hot Volkswagen outside the Right Steer for almost an hour past Candy Ann's quitting time. She hadn't emerged from work, and the cab that usually materialized to drive her home never appeared. The sun was low now, burning in through the car's rear window and gaining intensity in a fishbowl effect, like a magnifying glass used to start a fire. Nudger was the tinder.

Rather than burst into flame, he wiped his sleeve over his forehead, got out of the car, and trudged across the parking lot to the restaurant's entrance. The lot's blacktop, still holding the maximum heat of the day, adhered to his shoes and made slight sucking noises with each step.

He pushed through the Wild West, louvered swinging doors, then shoved open the pneumatic double-pane glass door, and stood just inside the blissfully air-conditioned Right Steer. Two elderly women, one of them with a cane, edged around him, studied the large wooden menu pegged to the wall, then moved toward the serving counter, where a yellow-uniformed cowgirl waited to take their orders and shoo them along toward the cash register like doggies toward the corral.

Nudger gazed over a wood partition at the crowded restaurant and the waitresses bustling about delivering steaks, refilling glasses, or wiping down tables. He didn't see Candy Ann.

When a young blond waitress drifted near to refill coffee mugs, Nudger leaned over the partition.

"Jodi," he said, noticing her name branded onto her uniform blouse, "is Candy Ann Adams still here?"

Jodi stopped and smiled at him, as if she were about to tell him that she was his waitress and if he needed anything just let her know and she'd be glad to serve him. But she said, "Candy Ann? She left a couple of hours ago. Had to pick up her car before someplace closed. Leastways, that's what she said." He caught a tone of resentment in her voice, as if Candy Ann's absence might be the reason all the other waitresses had to hustle around at double speed.

Nudger thanked her and walked back outside to cross the sticky parking lot to the Volkswagen.

He drove to Placid Grove Trailer Park, watching the miles tick away on the odometer. Four and a half miles exactly.

He saw no sign of anyone's presence in Candy Ann's trailer, no car parked nearby; only a gray squirrel that scurried across the trailer roof, then did a precarious tightrope act on the telephone-service wire and made for a nearby tree.

Vehicles were parked so that there was no place Nudger could wait in his car inside the trailer park without possibly arousing suspicion, so he drove back to Watson Road. He found a spot in the shade of some tall sycamores, then pulled the Volkswagen onto the shoulder where he could see the park entrance. After switching off the engine, he reached over and opened the passenger-side door to reap a little more breeze. The car's interior was hot to the touch.

Then he did what he spent too much time doing in this odd occupation that had chosen him. What he did in hotel lobbies, parking lots, bars, empty apartments, phone booths, and places too varied to classify.

He waited.

It was dark when she finally arrived. Nudger caught a glimpse of her gaunt profile as she turned her car in beneath the arched "Placid Grove" sign.

He started the Volkswagen and followed, keeping her car's bright red taillights in sight until they seemed to draw close together and disappeared as she made a right turn onto Tranquillity Lane in her final leg toward home.

He pulled to the side of the street and waited, giving her plenty of time to get inside, before he put the Volkswagen in gear and parked a short distance beyond her trailer.

As he walked up Tranquillity Lane in the dark, it seemed that the crickets were screaming with insane volume and intensity, the way they'd screamed the night he'd talked to Tom. Or maybe that was because the rest of the trailer park was so quiet; it was still too hot for anyone to be outside without good reason. Fireflies winked among the trailers, sending mysterious luminous signals, the only visible signs of life or motion.

Candy Ann's car, an old but glossy yellow Ford, was nosed in close to her trailer. On his way to the door, Nudger paused and scratched the hood with a key. Even in the dim light he could see that beneath the new yellow paint the car's color was dark green or black. He bent down and looked at the license plate. The number began with an *L*.

The crickets stopped screaming then, suddenly.

It took a few seconds for the silence to register with Nudger.

He was straightening up when one of the shadows in the corner of his vision suddenly gained substance and rushed at him.

Nudger started to yell in alarm, but he was hit hard in the side, momentarily knocking the breath from him and causing his injured rib to flare with pain.

He was on the ground. A large man loomed over him, leg drawn back to kick. Nudger rolled to his left, felt a shoe graze his hip. He scrambled to his feet, and a glancing blow scraped his neck and almost knocked him down.

The man rushed him again. This time Nudger sidestepped and drove a fist into the big man's stomach, heard a grunt more of irritation than of pain or breathlessness. Wow! The guy's midsection was hard enough to have hurt Nudger's fist. He was fit as a commando, wearing a dark long-sleeved shirt, with what looked like a knit ski mask pulled down to conceal his features.

Hot night for that, Nudger thought inanely, as the man grabbed the front of his shirt. Buttons shot like popped corn into the shadows.

Nudger tried to shove his assailant away, but the man barked a short half-grunt, half-scream and hacked down with the edge of his hand at Nudger's neck. The blow missed and glanced off his shoulder, struck the yellow hood of the car. Had to leave dents in both places.

Then the big man was up tight against him, using his weight, bending Nudger backward over the hood. He grabbed Nudger's hair and began beating his head on the smooth metal. More dents. It was making a hell of a racket, but probably not enough to arouse the neighbors and bring help. Or maybe it only seemed loud to Nudger. Pain exploded between his ears with each impact.

When the back of Nudger's head bounced particularly hard off the car, something must have jarred loose beneath the hood. The horn abruptly blared and kept howling.

The man straightened, glaring down like a specter through the ski mask's eyeholes, and Nudger recognized him.

He took a final swipe, breezing a fist past Nudger's face, then wheeled and ran into the darkness. He moved fast for his size.

Nudger heard his footsteps on the gravel road long after he lost sight of him.

Nudger stood up straight and gingerly traced the back of his head with his fingertips, then studied the fingers in the moonlight. There was no blood. Thank God the Ford didn't have a hood ornament.

He walked around to the driver's-side door and pulled the hood latch. Then he raised the hood, located the horn wires, and yanked them loose.

The blaring horn suddenly was silent.

" . . .*Fucking quiet!*" a man's voice yelled from the trailer across the street.

"It's okay now!" Nudger called back. "All fixed!" His head felt as if it were still bouncing off the hood. Only the cardboardlike thinness and pliability of the metal had saved him from serious injury. Thank you, Detroit.

He straightened his clothes, noticing that his pants were ripped at the knee. He knew he'd been lucky. The blaring horn had alerted the neighbors and saved him; his powerful attacker hadn't had time to inflict much damage.

"Who's out there?" a wavering voice called. "What's going on?"

Nudger turned and saw Candy Ann poised in the doorway of her trailer, her hand still on the knob so she could duck back inside and lock out the bogeyman if necessary.

"Me, Nudger," Nudger said, out of breath. "I'm what's going on." He waited for the ground to stop tilting, then moved into the light. A dull pain caromed around inside his skull.

"Then come on in," she said.

32

Candy Ann stood watching him walk toward the door. When their eyes locked, she tried a smile, but she couldn't quite manage her facial muscles, as if they'd become rigid and uncoordinated. In the yellow glare of reflected light streaming from the trailer, she appeared much older. The little-girl country look had deserted her; now she was an emaciated, grief-eroded woman, a country Barbie Doll whose features some evil child had lined with dark crayon. The shaded crescents beneath her eyes deprived them of their innocence. She was holding a glass that had once been a jelly jar. In it were two fingers of a clear liquid. Behind her on the table was a crumpled brown paper bag and a bottle of gin. The bottle was almost full, but it was obvious to Nudger when he caught a whiff of her breath that Candy Ann had been drinking before she arrived home.

"This is a surprise and a pleasure," she managed to say, still not smiling, trying a mannered country charm that fell far from the mark. "What in the world happened out there?"

"Someone was hanging around your car," Nudger said. "Maybe a hubcap thief. I scared him away."

She stood peering down at him from the top of the three steps into the trailer, still with her hand on the doorknob. Her thin body shifted uneasily, as if a strong wind were snatching at it.

He might be the bogeyman after all.

"I figured it out," Nudger told her.

Now she did smile, but it was fleeting, a sickly greenish shadow crossing her taut features. "You're a man of powerful persistence, Mr. Nudger. You surely don't know when to turn loose."

She stepped back and he followed her into the trailer. It was warm in there; something was wrong with the air conditioner.

"Hot as hell, ain't it," Candy Ann commented. Nudger thought that was apropos.

He found himself sitting across from her at the tiny Formica table, just as he and Tom had sat facing each other eleven days ago. She offered him a drink. He declined. She downed the contents of the jelly-jar glass and clumsily poured herself more gin, spilling some of it on the table. It was cheap gin but hundred proof, possibly strong enough to eat through the Formica.

"Now, what's this you've got figured out, Mr. Nudger?" There was something fearful and plaintive in the way she asked. She didn't want to, but she had to hear him say it. Had to share it.

"It's over four miles to the Right Steer Steakhouse," Nudger told her. "The waitresses there make little more than minimum wage, and there's no tipping, so cab fare to and from work has to take a big bite out of your salary, almost make a job there not worthwhile. But then you seem to go everywhere by cab. When I saw you leave Curtis' funeral in one, I realized that."

"Well, sure. My car's been in the shop."

"Your neighbors say it's been gone for months."

"I loaned it to a friend. She drove it a while, then she run it off the road into some trees and smashed it all up. I didn't have no collison insurance, so it took me some time to get it fixed. It was up on blocks where I had it towed. That's where it's been all this time, in the shop."

"I figured it might be," Nudger said, "after I found the money and wig."

She bowed her head slightly and took a fortifying sip of gin. "Money? Wig?"

"In the cardboard box above the ceiling panel in your bathroom."

"You been snooping, Mr. Nudger." There was more resignation than outrage in her voice.

"You're sort of skinny, but not a short girl," Nudger went on. "With a dark curly wig and a fake mustache, dressed similarly and sitting in a car, you'd resemble Curtis Colt enough to fool a dozen eyewitnesses who just caught a glimpse of you. It was a smart precaution for the two of you to take."

Candy Ann looked astounded. "Are you saying I was driving the getaway car at that liquor-store holdup?"

"Maybe. Then maybe you hired someone to play Tom and convince me he was Colt's accomplice and that they were far away from the murder scene when the trigger was pulled. I talked to some of your neighbors; they told me your car was a dark green Ford sedan. You were keeping the car hidden since the police had a partial description of it, then you had it painted yellow so you could begin driving it again."

Candy Ann ran the tip of her tongue along the edges of her protruding teeth. She thought for a moment before speaking.

"You're partway right. It's true that Curtis and Tom used my car for their holdups. That wig, it belongs to Tom."

"I doubt if Tom ever met Curtis. He's somebody you paid in stolen money or drugs to sit where you're sitting now and lie to me. And remember, he said he burned the wig after Curtis was arrested."

"If I was driving that getaway car, Mr. Nudger, and knew for sure Curtis was guilty, why would I have hired a private investigator to try to find a hole in the eyewitnesses' stories?"

"That bothered me for a while," Nudger said, "until I realized you weren't interested in clearing Curtis. What you were really worried about was Curtis Colt talking in prison. You didn't want

those witnesses' stories changed, you wanted them substantiated—
set in concrete so the witnesses wouldn't change their statements
even if Colt talked. And you wanted the police to learn about not-
his-right name Tom, to avert possible suspicion from you."

The crickets were raising a racket again outside, their shrill
ongoing scream the loudest sound in the baking trailer. Candy Ann
raised her head to look directly at Nudger with eyes that begged
and dreaded. She asked simply, "Why would I do that?"

"Because you were Curtis Colt's accomplice in all of his robberies. And when you hit the liquor store, he stayed in the car to
drive. You fired the shot that killed the old woman."

Candy Ann shook her head slowly, as if stunned. "Lordy, that's
crazy."

"Curtis was the one who fired the wild shot from the speeding
car," Nudger said. "I realized that when one of the witnesses,
Edna Fine, told me she saw an arm come out of the car to fire a
gun back toward the liquor store. She was looking at the car from
the left side. The driver's side. It was the driver's-side window
she'd seen the arm come out of to fire the shot. Curtis' arm. Which
was why tests indicated he'd fired a gun that night."

"Why, that just ain't so, Mr. Nudger. None of it."

"It's so. And you cozied up to Randy Gantner so you could
make him stand firm if the other witnesses did change their stories.
When it looked as if I might actually make progress, you would
have aroused curiosity if you'd simply called me off the case, so
you had Gantner hire one of his union strong-arm friends to beat
me up and try to scare me off it. When that failed, Gantner made
sure the other witnesses would stick to their stories; he even ter-
rorized Edna Fine by killing her pet. While I was following you,
waiting for you to get the car I was sure you must still have hidden
somewhere, Gantner was following me. Just now, outside, he realized how much trouble he was in, how much you'd lured him into
doing for you by playing up to his adolescent machismo, and he
tried again to use force to stop me." Nudger looked at the gin

bottle. He felt like taking a drink, but he didn't. "Did Gantner just hold you when you slept with him, Candy Ann?"

She didn't answer. She drained her glass and poured another drink into the jelly-jar glass, striking the neck of the bottle hard on the thick rim. It made a surprisingly sharp, flinty sound, as if sparks might fly.

"Colt never talked," Nudger said. "Not to the police, not to his lawyer, not even to a priest. Now that he's dead you can trust him forever, but I have a feeling you could have anyway. He loved you more than you loved him, and you'll have to live knowing he didn't deserve to die."

She looked down into her glass as if for answers and didn't say anything for a long time. Nudger felt a bead of perspiration trickle in a wild zigzag course down the back of his neck, like a tiny live thing crazy from the heat.

Then she said, "I didn't want to shoot that old man, but he didn't leave me no choice. Then the old woman come at me." She looked up at Nudger and smiled ever so slightly. It was a smile Nudger hadn't seen on her before; it sent a tingling coldness through him. There was a pinpoint center of darkness, the abyss of madness, in her eyes. "God help me, Mr. Nudger, I can't quit thinking about shooting that old woman. And about Curtis."

"You murdered her," Nudger said softly. "Then you murdered Curtis Colt by keeping silent and letting him die for you."

"I was scared," she said simply, in a flat voice.

"Everybody's scared most of the time."

"That's right, I suppose. But some of us are more scared than others, and with more reason."

Nudger kept silent, refusing to agree with her. She hadn't confided everything to Gantner, he was sure. Nudger was the only one who knew everything about her, and he wouldn't tell her what she longed to hear, wouldn't soothe her and give her what she needed to justify her actions. There had to be a measure of justice in all of this, had to be some balance to the world.

"You can't prove nothing," Candy Ann said, still with her ancient-eyed, eerie smile that had little to do with amusement.

"You're right," Nudger told her, "I can't. But I don't think legally proving it is necessary, Candy Ann. You said it: our thoughts are actually tiny electrical impulses in the brain. Curtis Colt rode the lightning all at once. With you, it will take years, but the destination is the same. I think you'll come to agree that his ride was easier."

She sat very still. She didn't answer. Wasn't going to.

Nudger stood up and wiped his damp forehead with the back of his hand. He felt sticky, dirty, confined by the low ceiling and near walls of the tiny, stifling trailer. He had to get out of there fast to escape the sensation that he was trapped.

He didn't say good-bye to Candy Ann when he walked out. She didn't say good-bye to him.

The last sound Nudger heard as he stepped down from the trailer was the clink of the bottle on the glass.

33

It was December, and frost had softly webbed the corners of Nudger's office window, when Hammersmith phoned and told him Candy Ann Adams had committed suicide.

All of Nudger's breath left him for an instant; something icy whispered in his ear. It hadn't taken as long as he'd thought; he could imagine Candy Ann old and guilt-ravaged, but it was difficult to imagine her dead.

"She was found in her bathtub with her radio," Hammersmith said. "The radio was on, she was off." Beneath his flipness lay an almost unfathomable sadness. Nudger knew Hammersmith as probably no one else did, knew how sarcasm and irony hid the real man, protected him from pain. But this time it wasn't enough protection.

"Maybe it was an accident," Nudger suggested, knowing better, knowing what had saddened Hammersmith.

"She left a note, Nudge. She admitted killing the old woman, and she admitted using you, and then Gantner, to try to make sure Curtis Colt burned for what she did. It was all the way you figured it last summer."

"What about Gantner?" Nudger asked, fastening a few more buttons on his sweater. The office was cold.

"He was telling the truth," Hammersmith said. "Candy Ann told him Colt had put her up to trying to get the witnesses to change their stories, that he'd shot the old woman and she was afraid of him and knew he'd kill her if he escaped execution and somehow got out of prison. That's how she talked Gantner and his strong-arm buddy into trying to scare you off the case when it looked as if you might get to the truth. I think Gantner only realized Colt was innocent, and Candy Ann was the killer, when he followed you around after the funeral and guessed what you'd figured out."

That was how Nudger had seen it. Hammersmith had questioned Gantner in July, trying to find out if Candy Ann had admitted the liquor-store killings. But Gantner was smart enough not to implicate himself as an accessory to murder and had denied knowing of Candy Ann's guilt. He'd been telling it straight, and there hadn't been enough evidence to bring charges against him.

Nudger could feel Hammersmith's grief and frustration flowing through the phone connection. Hammersmith was a cop, not a killer. But he'd helped to build a case against an innocent man, helped to send him out on the lightning.

"It's over," Nudger said. "Don't let it haunt you."

"It's over for Curtis Colt, too," Hammersmith said.

"He was driving the car," Nudger reminded Hammersmith. "He was involved."

"But he didn't pull the trigger," Hammersmith said. "He didn't kill anyone. The law did. And I'm the law." He fired up a cigar; Nudger could hear him slurping and puffing furiously on it. Hammersmith was getting mad, feeling the corrosiveness of what had happened eating into him, gnawing. "I don't buy that vigilante bullshit, Nudge. The man didn't deserve to die."

"He didn't," Nudger agreed. "But he wasn't perfect. Neither is the law, and neither are we."

Hammersmith was quiet for a moment. Then he said, "I better get busy, Nudge. Crime never takes time out. And I'm so popular. Every damn line on my phone is blinking. Every one."

Nudger wondered if that was true. He told Hammersmith not to be hard on himself and hung up.

He knew how Hammersmith would take this. He wouldn't go home and beat his wife or kick his dog or get drunk. He'd brood a while, then plunge ahead into his work, stay hard at it until time dulled memory and he reached some sort of acceptance of the past, a perspective he could live with rather than put his gun in his mouth and follow Candy Ann. Eating the gun, going out like Billy Abraham. Hammersmith wouldn't do that. He'd be all right, but it wouldn't be easy.

When word of Curtis Colt's innocence became public, Scott Scalla began to maneuver. He was no statesman, but when it came to raw politics, he could shuck and jive with the best. He was terribly upset over Colt's execution, his press secretary said, over and over. God only knew how much the governor had agonized over this. Scalla himself, interviewed after a Friends of God Christmas assembly, implied that there had been police incompetence, then a cover-up, in the Colt case. That's where the mistake had occurred, at a lower level, so that by the time the matter reached the governor's office, there was little Scalla could do but follow the letter of the law and not intercede in the execution. An innocent man was dead, and the governor of a great state had been made an unwitting accomplice, helplessly bound by law. The law had been subverted, perverted. Scalla promised an investigation. This mess in the legal process would be cleaned up.

But Scalla didn't really want an investigation. Not one that involved him. What he wanted was to leave the least damaging impression possible on voter consciousness, which he managed to do with the right succession of statements and images.

The investigation soon was shuffled from the state level down to the St. Louis Board of Police Commissioners conducting an interdepartmental investigation. Media attention had been usurped by bigger news, some of it manufactured for just that purpose, and the voting public had other things on its collective mind. And as the governor had promised, there *was* an investigation taking place.

All that was needed now was a scapegoat, someone to shoulder the entire burden of Colt's wrongful conviction and execution. A sacrificial name and face that would appease the public and close the case forever.

Someone expendable.

Who better than the officer who'd been in charge of the murder investigation? Homicide Lieutenant John Edward "Jack" Hammersmith.

Nudger wasn't as concerned as he might have been when he heard about the investigation of Hammersmith, and the lieutenant's suspension with pay. The Board of Commissioners knew the game; its members were under the gun themselves. And Nudger knew Hammersmith better than Scott Scalla did.

"It's okay, Nudge," Hammersmith said, when Nudger dropped by to see him at his house in Webster Groves. Though the temperature was in the forties, Hammersmith was sitting in a lawn chair under a leafless hundred-year-old oak in his backyard. He was wearing paint-spattered work pants and a red-and-black mackinaw and looked more sloppy-fat than he did in uniform. "I'm gonna be okay."

Nudger believed him. Hammersmith was, in the narrow range of his profession, as skilled and wily a politician as Scott Scalla. He could fade and feint with departmental bureaucracy, with the media, and with the Board of Police Commissioners, about whom Hammersmith knew more than they suspected.

Hammersmith got one of his horrendous cigars from his shirt pocket and lit it with a book match. "Wife won't let me smoke these in the house," he said.

"She probably doesn't want green drapes."

"By the way," Hammersmith said, "I got myself a good lawyer. Charles Siberling."

Nudger thought about Siberling fiercely chewing and spitting his way through the police-department legal process. He smiled. Hammersmith would indeed be okay. "Siberling's a good choice," he said. "You're hardly playing fair with the department."

Hammersmith beamed around his cigar, his blue eyes piercing through the putrid haze. "Boy, he's a slippery little bastard," he said in admiration. "Just like a goddamned barracuda with a briefcase. What a future he has."

"Pneumonia will be in my future," Nudger said, "if I don't get in out of this cold." The fog of his breath rose before his face.

Nudger had never seen Hammersmith do what he did then; he snubbed out a cigar half-smoked. "Come on into the house, Nudge. We'll have a few beers and bitch about the world in general."

An hour later, reassured about Hammersmith and sated by a ham sandwich and two Budweisers, Nudger returned to his apartment.

In his mail was his voter-registration confirmation, informing him of the date of the next election and the location of his polling place. The state was asking for a sales-tax increase to help fund highway maintenance. The bill's opponents claimed that the additional tax money actually would free other state money, which would be used to pay some of Scott Scalla's campaign obligations. "Money for pockets instead of potholes," their literature stated.

The state-paid TV spot that was played repeatedly was a scene in which a young family's station wagon hit a pothole, flew out of control, and burst into flames. Only the father, who'd been driving, survived, though not very happily. It was a gloomy situation anyone born of woman would vote to prevent.

The bill was expected to pass by a wide margin.

Nudger tossed the registration card and campaign literature into the wastebasket and decided not to vote.

Then he walked to the living room window, stood staring out at the murky, snow-pregnant winter sky, and changed his mind. That was what people like Scott Scalla relied on, people like Nudger not voting. Nudger would vote this time, and he'd keep on voting.

Maybe someday it would make a difference.

Maybe Charles Siberling would run for governor.

34

Nudger lay with Claudia in the morning light in her bedroom. He was on his back, beneath the blanket and sheet, while she lay on top of the covers, still breathing deeply. Everything had become good between them again, Nudger thought, though not as good as it had been before their newly defined relationship. He wasn't sure if Claudia was seeing other men. He never asked, fearful of the answer.

She sighed, propped herself up on one elbow, then swiveled to sit on the edge of the mattress. Nudger watched her with the familiar awe. Her lean body was breathtaking in the soft light. Half an hour ago his groin had ached for her, and now it was his heart. A compartmentalization the women's liberation movement would

frown upon with unplucked brows. Maybe they were right; sometimes Nudger felt as extinct as one of those dinosaurs with two
brains, each of which provided disastrously poor judgment.

Claudia stood up and turned to look down at him. "I don't see
how you can bear to stay beneath those covers," she said. "The
radiator keeps it at two thousand degrees in here."

"I'm cold," he told her. "Cold's a subjective thing, even at
two thousand degrees."

She shook her head, and he watched her walk away, into the
bathroom. Some walk.

The shower hissed and gurgled for a while, then Claudia returned, still toweling herself dry. There were goose bumps on her
arms and thighs, and her flesh was reddened where she'd rubbed
too hard with the rough towel.

As she began to dress, she asked, "How's Hammersmith
doing?" She'd always liked Hammersmith, and she knew how
what had happened worked on him.

"Things have returned to his idea of normal," Nudger said.

"He must know some important people."

"Better yet, he knows *about* some important people."

The Board of Police Commissioners, after an appropriate length
of time, had exonerated Hammersmith. They had become so in-
censed at Siberling that they suggested it was the judicial system
that had been at fault in the Colt conviction and execution. Siberling blamed police procedures, politics, the sun, the moon, and the
stars, everything and everyone other than Hammersmith. The buck
that had stopped at Hammersmith had been broken down into
small change that no one cared about.

The problem was—as with Claudia and Nudger—things would
never be quite the same for Hammersmith. That's what life seemed
to come down to, losing some small part of yourself here, another
there, inching toward icy darkness.

Claudia was standing hipshot in her Levi's, buttoning a white
cotton blouse. Nudger liked her best when she dressed plainly to

set off her subtle beauty. Simply looking at her gave him a sensation of contentment and wholeness. He needed her more than he'd planned. So much more. He thought about Candy Ann and Curtis Colt, and wondered if love was a trap for everyone. His and Claudia's lives wouldn't go on forever; was it any wonder he was selfish about her? Okay, more than selfish. Downright greedy and possessive.

"Why don't we get away this weekend?" he suggested. "Drive somewhere and find blissful isolation? Maybe rent a cabin."

She missed a button. "I can't. I've got plans for this weekend."

"The entire weekend?"

She nodded, turned away from him, and began brushing her hair. Their eyes met in the dresser mirror. She looked away.

"With someone of my gender?" Nudger asked.

"Yes."

Nudger's heart suddenly weighed so much he didn't think he could budge. Claudia's image in the mirror seemed to recede, change, as if he were watching her through wavering, distorting glass.

"I really don't understand how you can stay beneath that sheet and blanket," she said, "as hot as it is. You must be crazy."

He listened to the sighing, faintly crackling strains of the brush passing through her long hair. It was almost like the sound of sizzling, high-voltage current, of dwindling time.

"Not crazy," Nudger said, "cold. Colder than before."

But he threw back the covers and struggled out of bed into his world.

Some people you couldn't crush.

BESTSELLING BOOKS FROM TOR

THE BEST IN SUSPENSE

- ☐ 50105-5 CITADEL RUN by Paul Bishop $4.95
  50106-3 Canada $5.95

- ☐ 54106-5 BLOOD OF EAGLES by Dean Ing $3.95
  54107-3 Canada $4.95

- ☐ 51066-6 PESTIS 18 by Sharon Webb $4.50
  51067-4 Canada $5.50

- ☐ 50616-2 THE SERAPHIM CODE by Robert A. Liston $3.95
  50617-0 Canada $4.95

- ☐ 51041-0 WILD NIGHT by L. J. Washburn $3.95
  51042-9 Canada $4.95

- ☐ 50413-5 WITHOUT HONOR by David Hagberg $4.95
  50414-3 Canada $5.95

- ☐ 50825-4 NO EXIT FROM BROOKLYN by Robert J. Randisi $3.95
  50826-2 Canada $4.95

- ☐ 50165-9 SPREE by Max Allan Collins $3.95
  50166-7 Canada $4.95

Buy them at your local bookstore or use this handy coupon:
Clip and mail this page with your order.

Publishers Book and Audio Mailing Service
P.O. Box 120159, Staten Island, NY 10312-0004

Please send me the book(s) I have checked above. I am enclosing $_____
(please add $1.25 for the first book, and $.25 for each additional book to
cover postage and handling. Send check or money order only — no CODs.)

Name _____

Address _____

City _____ State/Zip _____

Please allow six weeks for delivery. Prices subject to change without notice.

ELIZABETH PETERS

THE BEST IN SCIENCE FICTION